BROKEN HART

A CROSS CREEK SMALL TOWN NOVEL

KELLY COLLINS

BOOK NOOK PRESS

Copyright © 2020 by Kelley Maestas
All rights reserved.
No part of this book may be reproduced in any form or by any electronic or mechanical means, including information storage and retrieval systems, without written permission from the author, except for the use of brief quotations in a book review.

Cover design by Sly Fox

Edits by Show Me Edits

FOREWORD

Dear Reader,

I'm so excited to bring you the Cross Creek novels. If you've read my bestselling Aspen Cove series, you met the Lockhart Brothers in One Hundred Promises. I hope you fall in love with Noah, Bayden, Ethan, and Quinn. Welcome to Cross Creek where anything is possible and love always wins.

Happy reading,
Kelly

CHAPTER ONE

NOAH

Cross Creek wasn't a metropolis, but with a population of 2,500, I should have been able to escape three of the residents—my brothers—at least for a single night.

Sitting at a table in Roy's Bar, amongst many of the other less annoying residents, I brought my beer to my lips as my brothers entered and walked my way. Quinn dropped into the seat beside me. Ethan and Bayden—Quinn's fraternal twin—sat across the table and signaled for beers.

Quinn clapped me on the back. "You're extra broody tonight." I lifted both shoulders, then let them sag as if the strain of a dozen bags of concrete weighted them down. This time of year always hit me hard, and it amazed me that my brothers didn't get it.

"I'm not broody."

"He totally is," Quinn spoke directly to Bayden, who ignored both of us as Angie walked by. Bayden leaned over, watching the sway of her hips as she passed.

"Don't even think about it." Ethan lifted his gaze from his tablet, where he was likely jotting down ideas for our next big construction project and looked at Bayden. He snapped his fingers in front of Bayden's face but got his hand swatted away. "She's all wrong for you, bro."

The three of them gawked at Angie as she walked away. I wasn't sure what she had that made them drool like horny teenage boys. I guess living in a small town made fresh meat enticing. Angie hadn't been here long, but she didn't seem too interested in dating, especially not my obnoxious brothers. I tossed back the rest of my drink; any other night, it would be one and done, but I had a rough day and my brothers are driving me crazy, so tonight would be a double down—down my throat.

"Why'd you cut out early today?" Quinn turned to look at me.

"You guys could handle it." Old Roy walked up with my brothers' beers. He owned the bar and could be anyone's grandfather with his white hair and watery blue eyes. He was a good guy, too—one whose colorful stories were a legend in this tight-knit community.

"Changing of the guard?" Quinn asked, glancing around at the lack of waiters and waitresses. Roy rarely ran drinks to tables unless he was the only one to do it, so the assumption was the next shift was clocking in.

Roy's deep voice was slow and measured. "Yep. Training a new waitress tonight." He left quickly as another table hailed him.

My brothers settled into their seats, and Bayden and Quinn took long pulls off their beers. Their mannerisms were identical, even though they weren't.

We often hung out here for drinks after work, which was why quitting time was my favorite part of the day. Usually, we'd haul ass over here and bullshit about everything and nothing. Tonight, I didn't feel much like talking.

"Who'd he sweet talk into working here?" Ethan scanned the bar.

I remained unfazed. As long as they could pull a beer and deliver it, who cared who Roy hired?

"What's wrong with working here?" Quinn asked defensively.

"Nothing, but—"

Quinn elbowed Ethan, "I'm messing with you. Lighten up. What's gotten into you guys today? You're all so damn glum." He didn't get much of a response, and with a sigh, he lifted his beer. "To Tuesday night."

A few tables down, Gypsy lifted her glass. "Are you boys being troublemakers again?" She wasn't one to blend in with her bright yellow and orange tie-dyed shirt. Her long gray hair hung loose to her waist in thick waves, and her bright-green eyes sparkled with mischief. Gypsy was a Woodstock leftover who never got the message that flower power and groovy were over decades ago.

"Yep, stirring things up as usual," Quinn lifted his mug in salute, spilling at least a sip over the edge.

Ethan's attention left his tablet, and he focused on the door. "Look who came to join the party."

Quinn ignored him, instead, continuing his conversation with Gypsy. Bayden glanced over his shoulder and stiffened. It was a Mom-walked-in-and-caught-you-in-the-candy-bowl kind of reaction.

Interesting.

Miranda—the new sheriff—stepped over the threshold. She pulled her hat off and nodded at Roy.

Bayden appeared to perk up, and I wondered if there was something between him and the sheriff. Bayden was Quinn's opposite in nearly every way, despite them being twins. His dark hair and sky-blue eyes weren't the only things that made him different. His close-lipped, quiet demeanor meant he kept things close to his vest. Given Ethan's words, I wasn't the only one who thought there might be something between our younger brother and the pretty new sheriff. Even though Angie had caught his eye earlier, it was obvious who had his full attention now.

Roy and Miranda shared a few words while I took in her five-foot six-ish frame. With her inky hair and almond-shaped eyes, she had an exotic air about her. Her fair skin didn't seem to soak up the sunshine like most of us, and her high cheekbones gave her a regal look.

While she appeared delicate, there was something fierce about her.

As if she read my mind, her dark gaze moved toward me then flicked to Bayden before returning to Roy.

Maybe there *was* something between them.

I took a swig of my beer and watched my brother study her.

"Don't make me show you a good time." Quinn's casual flirting with Gypsy brought a tittering laugh from the older woman.

"Boy, you wouldn't know what to do with me. Besides, you need some sweet thing who's your age." On the tail end of Gypsy's words, Angie walked to our table once more. Her brown eyes traced over every one of us, and we all leaned away from her except Bayden, who stayed focused on Miranda and didn't seem to notice Angie at all this time.

"Hey, boys." Angie paused.

Ethan was quick to speak up. "Hey, Angie, how are—"

"What's Benji doing here?" Bayden growled the words, and we all glanced in the door's direction. Benji, the local journalist for the Creekside Sentinel, stopped Miranda to talk to her, but she seemed less than thrilled.

"You know he likes to write stories on every new person in town, but Miranda's been dodging him like a pro." Quinn sounded proud of the sheriff.

Bayden turned and scowled, then lowered his beer to the table with a thump. There was definitely something going on with him and Miranda, if only in his mind for now. Was this flirtatious thing with Angie just a game? Was he trying to make the sheriff jealous?

Without a word about any of it, I finished my beer and

signaled for another. Roy caught my eye and nodded before heading back to the bar.

The back of my neck prickled, and the air took on that electric charge that usually came right before a fight or a wicked storm. I smoothed my hand over my skin and took in the room. Nobody seemed like they were looking for a scuffle, and the last time I saw the sky, it was clear.

At the bar, a familiar-looking young woman smoothed her hands down the front of her apron with an unsure slowness. Her white-blonde hair framed her face and tumbled down her back. When she lifted her head, I jolted like someone had kicked me in the dangly bits.

Her brilliant, ocean-blue eyes locked on Roy with a hint of relief, and a smile crossed her full, cherry-red lips.

She said something I couldn't hear, and every bit of me tried to tune in to listen to her voice. Her fingertips brushed her cheekbone and shifted her hair back as she focused on Roy. Whatever he said had her nodding, and she gracefully tied her hair up with an elastic band she had wound around her wrist. Getting it up and out of her face only drew more attention to her beautiful features. She laughed at something Roy said, and the sweet lilting sound ribboned through me.

My heart stilled, then burst forth like it had been shocked with paddles—paddles covered in barbed wire that shredded me to bits.

What was Kandra doing here?

As I looked at my empty mug, I came face-to-face with the realization that she was the girl Roy mentioned.

"I know we are young, but I have never been more sure of anything in my life, Kandra." I got down on one knee and looked up at her, "Will you marry me?" She had tears rolling down her face, and I thought I was about to be the happiest man in the world. Then she said, "Noah, I love you, but I can't stay here in Cross Creek. I have dreams. I want to see the world, I want to be a photog-

rapher, and I can't do that if I'm here." Then, *without so much as a second thought, she left, and I was there, kneeling like a chump and holding a ring I couldn't return.*

"Noah?" The tone and inflection told me it wasn't the first time Quinn said my name.

"Yeah?" I locked down my emotions, hoping the shock didn't show on my face, but it was too late. He tapped both Ethan and Bayden to get their attention.

All eyes on him, he nodded toward the bar. "Is that..." Quinn seemed at a loss for words.

I looked at her again, hating every second of my life for the current moment. This was an awful dream—a nightmare—a cruel trick played by the powers that be. There was no way this could be happening. I refused to give in or let my brothers see how she still affected me.

Kandra laughed, her straight white teeth just as bright and perfect as they were back then.

Roy showed her the taps, and she filled a glass but didn't tilt it as he taught her. The foamy head overflowed and spilled to the counter. She jumped back, and the glass slipped from her hand and shattered against the bar.

Her cheeks turned crimson, and a string of apologies fell from her lips.

My insides simmered, working up to a full boil. *Where are my apologies?*

Roy calmly helped her clean up the mess. The second attempt went better as she tipped the glass and triumph shone in her beautiful features.

"Is that Kandra?" Quinn finally found his voice.

"Damn." Ethan finished his beer and signaled Roy for another. "I'm not interested, but even I can see time has been kind to her. She's even more beautiful now." A *thunk* sounded under the table.

"Ouch." He glared at Quinn. "What the—" Our brother must have kicked him.

"Don't even think about it," Quinn said to Ethan, before turning to me.

"Don't worry about it." Kandra and I were old news. She moved on when she realized I couldn't give her the life she wanted, so it didn't matter that she was back. Not one bit. "You can have her." I finished my beer.

"You can't have her," Quinn said to Ethan before turning to me. "Noah, you loved her, man. Maybe her coming back is a sign."

"Yeah, it's red, octagonal, and says *STOP* in big white letters." I glowered into my empty glass. I would not let Kandra back into my life. I swore back then I'd never hand anyone the tools to gut me ever again.

"Come on, Noah. Nobody's falling for it." Quinn's forgotten beer rested between his hands while he leaned across the table to get closer.

"There's nothing to fall for." I refused to look at her again for fear that something would give me away.

Quinn snorted. "You're still in love with her."

I shook my head. "Why don't you play matchmaker somewhere else? I'm not interested." I jerked my chin in Bayden's direction.

Quinn had to know he and Miranda were making eyes at each other, but Quinn ignored his twin and scrutinized me instead. "Nice try. You don't get to deflect this."

"There's nothing to deflect because there's nothing there." He didn't get it. Kandra and I were a dead end. There was nothing between us but bitter history, and no amount of probing, pestering, or pleading on his part could change that.

"Okay. Then you won't mind if I do this." Quinn stood up, cupped his hands around his mouth, and called out, "Another round, please."

"You're a dick." I wanted to kick him, but when I swung my boot, he stepped back.

He grinned. "I'm gonna hit the head."

Bayden stood up and moved in Angie's direction, but Ethan shoved him back into his chair. "Don't even think about it."

My brothers glared at each other.

"What's this sudden interest in Angie?" I asked.

Bayden looked from me to Ethan to Miranda. "Maybe I'm interested … or maybe I'm trying to make someone jealous."

"Which is it?" Ethan grumbled.

"What's it matter to you?"

"Sorry, guys." Roy dropped off our beers, ending the sibling exchange, and rushed away.

"Guess the universe is giving you a break since Roy delivered the drinks." Ethan didn't take his eyes off Bayden. There was something feral and territorial in them. They were like two dogs going after the same bone.

I snorted. "A break? Yeah, right." Kandra didn't come to the table this time, but what about next time? What about tomorrow? There was no way I could avoid her forever. Unless she got fired, but even then, I'd probably just bump into her around town. If I was truly lucky, she would move away again.

Bayden stood up and walked toward Angie.

Ethan tried to grab him again, but he evaded capture.

"He's tenacious," I said.

Ethan turned to face me. "He's a pain in the ass." He took a drink of his beer. "You never told us why you cut out early today."

I was glad to steer the conversation in a direction that wasn't Kandra. "It's two years tomorrow." I didn't need to remind him, because he already knew.

He lifted his head. "You visit him?"

It was what I did. I sat down every year next to his granite headstone and talked to my dad.

"I should have known." Ethan sounded disappointed. "You know, you can talk to us."

We'd been over this before. "I know. Thank you."

"You don't have to suffer alone." The raw note in his voice said he was grieving too. Because I was the oldest and had more years with dad, I think I took it the hardest.

This time of the year was difficult for all of us, and we dealt with it in our own private ways.

I withdrew, Ethan pretended nothing happened, Bayden grew sullen, and Quinn ... well, I had no idea how he handled things because nothing ever seemed to faze him. Though I knew it had devastated him, he seemed to have bounced back rather nicely.

"Thanks." I didn't know what else to say.

He seemed to sober up as he watched Bayden talk to Angie. "Two years," he muttered under his breath, more to himself than to me.

Time marched on as if our entire world hadn't been shaken to the core by the loss. Only two people had ever broken me; one couldn't help it, and the other was pulling beers at the taps. Seeing Kandra was an aftershock I didn't need today.

CHAPTER TWO

KANDRA

There's a saying that a person should never cross the same bridge twice, but what if the only open bridge leads to Cross Creek and the only job I can find lands me in Roy's?

Stinging bile backed up in my throat, singeing my tonsils, and my chest burned like I'd taken a shot of molten lava. Leaning a hip against the bar, I sucked in a deep breath as the wave of nausea eased and then reared back up with a vengeance. My hands wouldn't stop shaking as a case of nerves hit me hard.

I'd already broken one glass, but thankfully Roy was a kind man who encouragingly told me to try again.

I was determined to make the best of my new start in my old hometown.

"Table three needs a beer and a white wine." Roy hurried off, and I turned to stare at the liquor wall. I glanced over my shoulder at table three and instantly recognized Norman and Ethel. A smile crossed my lips. Knowing the old couple since birth, I guessed Ethel would want something fresh and fruity, while Norman probably wanted something bitter to match his disposition. He was always a prickly one. Quickly filling the glasses and moving carefully so I didn't break something else, I carried them to the table.

Ethel's sparkling eyes lit up when she saw me. "Is that little Kandra Sullivan?"

I smiled and placed their drinks in front of them. "Not so little anymore."

Norman snorted. "The girl's all grown up, Ethel."

"She's still a baby to me." Ethel's kind tone and warm smile made me feel welcomed home. She stood up and tugged me to her ample bosom for a warm hug. "How is your mother?"

"She's good." It was merely a conversation starter since Ethel had seen more of my mother in the last decade than I had. *Ten years ... had it really been that long?*

"Better now that her baby is home, I'm sure." Ethel gave me another squeeze, then sat back down. "Sit with us." She patted the worn seat beside her, but I shook my head. Scanning for Roy, I spotted him wink and then smile at me.

"I'm supposed to be working." I laid my index finger over my lips and made a *shh* sound. "Don't tell my boss I'm over here talking to the cutest couple in the place."

"Oh, you're so sweet!" Ethel laughed as Norman guzzled his beer.

"You know, in my day, we'd drink these in the boat while fishing in Aspen Cove." His gaze misted over.

Ethel touched his hand. "You can go fishing if you want, dear." Her sweet voice moved through me like warm syrup.

He eyed her with a confused look on his face. "Why the hell would I want to do that? It's cold out there on the water, and the damn fish don't bite no more. I went for the beer, anyway."

I giggled because I hadn't realized how much I missed the people in this town, even the crotchety ones. Time had a way of softening the hard edges of life.

"You have a beer." She nodded at his hand, and he looked down at it.

He took another drink, and Ethel pressed her lips together and then shook her head. "Did you meet anyone special while you were away?" she asked.

"That's something we'll have to talk about later," I said, already retreating. "I think Roy just hollered at me." He hadn't, but I wanted to avoid any talk about me and men. There was no use airing my dirty laundry, that wasn't my style. I was more of a suffer in silence kind of girl.

"We're glad you're back." Ethel's eyes crinkled at the corners. "You'll have to meet my grandson, I imagine he's about your age now."

Norman let out a loud noise that sounded something like, "Huh?"

Ethel leaned forward. "I'm saying she should meet our grandson." On a scale of one to ten, with ten being the loudest, Ethel had pitched to a seven.

"Which one?" His loud, gravelly voice didn't seem out of place in the bar. Over at her table, Gypsy laughed and talked to another group while several guys sang to the jukebox. Everyone was jockeying to be heard.

Ethel leaned toward her husband an inch more. "Roger."

Norman shook his head. "The kid wouldn't be into her."

Ethel snapped back like she'd been slapped.

Norman continued. "Trust me, she's not his type. She's got a job and a brain."

"How about Kingston?" She wasn't giving up.

"He's too young for her. Let the woman meet someone on her own, Ethel, don't play matchmaker." He downed his beer, and I picked up the empty glass.

"Another?" I asked, relieved for the chance to slip away.

"Huh?" He stared at me like he hadn't heard what I said, and it dawned on me that it wasn't the din of the bar, but Norman was hard of hearing.

I wiggled his glass, and he nodded.

"Do you need another wine?" I asked Ethel.

The thick scent of garlic and butter hit my nose, causing my stomach to twist. *Not garlic. Please, not garlic.* Over the last few weeks I'd found I couldn't tolerate the smell. I held my breath and waited for her answer.

"No, dear." Ethel lifted her nose in the air and inhaled. "Some of Roy's famous garlic knots would be wonderful, though."

"Garlic knots," Norman said, holding up two fingers. "Did you want some too?" he asked his wife. She sighed and crossed her arms, a knowing smile on her face. Without missing a beat, he glanced up at me and lifted another finger, "Three orders. The lady would like some too."

I laughed as I left the table. They were adorable and had the kind of love I longed for. The sort of relationship I thought I'd had, but I'd been wrong.

With efficiency, I refilled Norman's beer. When I dropped it back at their table, I caught them deep in conversation.

"Forty years of marriage, and we still have things to talk about." Ethel squeezed his hand.

"That's amazing."

"We're going to take a pottery class. You should join us. It would give you a chance to meet new people." Ethel's hopeful expression tugged at my heart.

"Oh, I don't know. I already broke a glass." I gestured over my shoulder, my cheeks heating as I thought about my mistake. "Maybe I should stay away from pottery." I couldn't help but notice the adoring look on Norman's face as he stared at his wife. I'd give anything to have someone look at me like that.

"Oh, don't you worry, girl. We'll keep you from breaking

things." Ethel chuckled, and I tried to think of a diplomatic way out of the invitation.

"Let the girl get back to work." Norman winked at me. "I think you owe us some knots."

I breathed a sigh of relief at the save.

"We'll touch base soon," Ethel said with a double wink, not to be outdone by her husband.

"Let her catch her breath before you go pushing boys on her. As pretty as she is, she likely has enough admirers." The words were barely out of Norman's mouth when a familiar voice sounded behind me.

"Kandra? Is that you?"

I smoothed a trembling hand down the front of my apron, put on my game face smile, and spun around.

Benji's curly brown hair had lengthened a bit and sprung away from his head a good three or four inches. His brown eyes bored into mine, and he stepped in and wrapped me in a tight hug.

"Welcome back."

I patted his shoulder awkwardly.

He stepped away and took both my hands in his. Excitement crackled like electricity in his eyes, and his warm fingers squeezed mine.

"It's good to see you." I gave a smile, hoping I sounded sincere. It wasn't that I didn't like Benji, it's that I didn't have the energy to deal with him.

"It's so good." He pulled me into another tight hug.

I stood there, stiff and uncomfortable, until his arms loosened. He stepped back and planted both hands on my shoulders. "We have to get together soon."

"Sure," I nodded, "but I'm working right now, so I should get back to it." Flashing a bright smile I didn't feel inside, I tried to shrug him off and leave, but his fingertips tightened, holding me captive. I met his stare head-on.

"Let me give you my number." His happy expression seemed frozen on his face, and a chill swept down my spine.

"That would be great." I passed him a napkin from my apron pocket, and he stared at it like I'd given him a germ infested rag.

"Don't you have a cell phone?"

Thinking fast, I nodded. "Yeah, but I'm not allowed to have it at work, so it's turned off and in my locker." I didn't like lying, but something about Benji seemed off. Upon reflection, something about him was always off.

"Can you get table eight another round?" Roy's voice was like a life preserver hitting the open ocean while I was drowning in the depths.

"Of course. Sorry for standing around." I smiled at Benji. "I have to go. Don't want to get fired on my first day." Before he could respond, I rushed off, with Roy a step behind me.

"Thank you." I wasn't sure why I was thanking him, but it seemed right.

"No worries. If I didn't step in and do something, table eight was going to." He offered me the tray of beers, and I balanced it, praying I wouldn't drop anything.

Focused on my task, it took a moment for me to realize what he'd said. If he hadn't stepped in, table eight would have. *Who was at table eight?*

I tilted my chin up high and scanned the tables. When my eyes landed on eight, my blood froze to Ice in my veins, and my legs stopped working. I stood there, staring at him. *Noah.*

Was he the one who would have stepped in if Roy hadn't?

His bright blue eyes met mine. The contrast of his dark hair and light eyes had always mesmerized me, but the boy I'd known in school had grown into a man—a handsome man, though he'd always been dangerously good-looking.

The slight curl to his lips and the cold hue of his eyes hit me like a tidal wave. Again, that drowning sensation washed over me, and I gasped in a breath.

Somehow I managed to coax my legs into moving and walked toward him, but every step might as well have been one closer to my undoing. I slogged forward like I was approaching a hangman's noose, ready to pay for all my crimes. Crimes I committed against Noah. Not literal, law-breaking ones, but crimes of the heart—crimes of love.

That day played in my mind like a high definition movie.

"Noah, I love you, but I can't stay here in Cross Creek. I have dreams. I want to see the world, I want to be a photographer, and I can't do that if I'm here." Walking away from him was the hardest thing I had ever done, but I couldn't risk staying and then resenting him if I couldn't pursue my dreams. An ocean rained from my eyes as I left him there by the creek, holding a ring that I didn't even look at.

My cheeks stung red hot as his gaze moved over me like he was taking stock and then met mine again. That cruel chill still shone brightly from his eyes. He wasn't the only Lockhart gawking; his brothers were studying me too.

I'd been in love with Noah, but Ethan, Quinn, and Bayden had always treated me like family. Seeing them made me realize how much I missed them.

An uncomfortable tingle danced over my skin, leaving undulating waves of prickling heat and icy chill behind. I imagined that this is what sticking a fork in a light socket felt like. My chest contracted painfully like it was trying to squeeze the life from me. My stomach twisted into knots that were less fluffy and airy than Roy's garlic treats.

A cruel smile tugged the corners of Noah's lips as I approached with the speed of a slug.

While he had every right to be, was he still angry at me after all these years? Something about Roy's statement wasn't meshing in my brain. I couldn't entertain the thought of him standing up to Benji for me while still being mad at me for the past.

Sure, Noah had always been a good guy, but would he defend the honor of a woman who had no honor to speak of?

Dark spots swam before my eyes, and I adjusted the tray in my aching arm while begging myself not to faint.

I was back in Cross Creek, freshly dumped, alone, and standing in front of my first love, who stared at me like I was something someone had dragged in on the bottom of their shoe.

CHAPTER THREE

NOAH

"She's almost here." Quinn's voice stayed in rhythm with his tap on Ethan's shoulder. Bayden sat sullenly after his conversation with Angie, but my eyes were on Kandra.

Tomorrow was the anniversary of the most tragic loss of my life, and it coincided with the woman I'd loved—the one who tore my heart out—showing back up in our hometown.

Could my day get any worse?

What next? Was I about to fall out of my chair from a heart attack? An aneurysm, maybe?

I finished my beer and watched her approach. Her "deer in the headlights" expression didn't change one bit as she inched our way. She pressed her full, red lips together into a tight line, then released them. When the blood rushed back, they appeared redder —the color of succulent overripe strawberries.

Kandra knew all the tricks of the trade. The woman who left wanting to be a *photographer* became a model instead, so the whole lip thing was no accident. How many men fell for those soulful eyes and kissable lips?

I scrubbed my face with my palm. What did it matter? Everything she ever told me, everything she'd claimed to aspire to, was all bullshit. I could put a rock in a pretty box, but at the end of the day, it was still just a rock. Pretty on the outside doesn't mean the inside matches.

I had nothing against attractive women or modeling as a profession, but I didn't like being lied to, manipulated, or tricked by someone who claimed to love me.

Her aquamarine eyes locked on to my face and silently begged me not to make a scene. How was it that, after all these years, I could still read her expressions, but she obviously never really knew me if she thought I was the kind of guy to cause trouble.

"Be cool." Quinn elbowed Ethan, who let out a stunned grunt. "But not too cool. She's Noah's, remember."

"She's not mine," I grumbled under my breath. Maybe she had been once when we were kids. Back then, I'd given her my heart, but Kandra Sullivan didn't love men for who they were, she loved men for what they could give her, and I failed to give her the things she thought she needed, so she abandoned me.

She was so close her sweet perfume tickled my nose. It was something citrusy, like tangerines mixed with peaches.

"We have to be at work early." Ethan's chair scraped the wooden floor as he pushed back and stood up. I glanced at him as he tossed cash onto the table—more than enough to cover his beers. With a nod, he walked toward the door.

Bayden downed the rest of his beer, thumped the mug on the tabletop, and rose. "I need to get home and grab a shower. I've got a hot date tonight."

"Yeah, with your right hand." Quinn's teasing earned him a sharp glare.

Bayden paid his portion and left a tip before heading for the door right on Ethan's heels.

Quinn flashed me a salute. "I just remembered, I have plans

tonight." He laid a few bills on the table while his gaze slid side to side like the eyes on the Kit-Cat clock. "Have a good one."

Without another word, or giving me a chance to say anything, he all but ran for the door, leaving me alone.

I turned in time to see Kandra stop in front of me. She inhaled, inflating her ribs—no doubt to make me notice her assets, which were still nice, but I wasn't going to get sucked into her games ever again.

Standing there, she gripped the tray so tightly her fingers blanched. Her lips curved into a smile that trembled at the corners.

"They sure scattered in a hurry." Her voice wobbled at first, but quickly gained confidence. "Like mice running from a cat."

The attempt at humor fell flat, and I didn't respond. What was there to say? Yeah, my brothers took off and left me because they didn't know what really happened between us when we dated. They didn't know the truth, and they thought there was some chance we'd get back together. They couldn't be more wrong.

She shifted her weight and set a beer in front of me but looked at the three still on her tray. "Want me to take these back?"

I lifted a shoulder. I didn't give a damn what she did. I considered drinking all four. If I overdid it, I'd have to have someone drive me home. My brothers would gladly pick me up at home in the morning and drop me at my truck.

She seemed unsure and shifted her weight back to her left side. Her tongue slid across her lower lip, and I glanced away. Why was she trying to make small talk? We weren't friends, and I didn't want to engage with her. Hell, I'd have been happy if she never came back to Cross Creek in the first place.

Now I'd have another constant reminder of our failed relationship. I picked up my beer and took a drink, looking into the glass instead of at her.

"I'll just leave them." She set the drinks down and tucked the tray under her arm. "So, how have you been?"

I stared up at her. Why would she even ask me that?

Her eyes widened. Then she glanced over her shoulder at Roy. Quickly, as if worried she would change her mind, she sat down. Stiff as a board, and clearly uncomfortable, she said, "I'm sorry. Look, I'm having a rough day. I didn't think I'd ever come back, and I certainly never thought I'd work in a bar, but here I am." She spread her hands and let out a chuckle that held no humor. "I never imagined this was how we'd bump into one another, but this is my life, and I'm trying to make the best of it. Can we call a truce?"

She thrust a hand in my direction, and I studied her, considering her words.

Her brave smile wavered as the seconds ticked by, but I didn't take her hand. She lowered it a fraction of an inch as her eyes misted over.

I might not have shaken her hand, but I swallowed hard. "The beers are paid for, so it's fine if you leave them. Can you add garlic knots to my order?" Internally, I heard my mother's admonishing tone and added, "*Please*."

Relief flooded her features, but her shoulders drooped. "Garlic knots." As she said the words like she was committing them to memory, she recoiled. "Be back with those in a few minutes." With that, she walked away.

"So, are you two ... you know?" Benji's voice hit my ears before he arrived at the table. "Are you going to rekindle the old flame?" His eyes ate up Kandra like she was a snack.

I wanted to hit him. Why she put up with him back in high school was a mystery, and why she dealt with him now blew my mind.

"Keep walking," I snarled.

I never liked Benji. He put me on edge, and the way he

demanded interviews of new people in town and put their stories in the paper always had a predatory feel. He had the first say, and that gave others their initial impression, which didn't seem fair. Shouldn't people be judged on their own merit?

Benji held both hands, palms up, to his shoulders in a classic sign of surrender. "Sorry. I'm going." He walked off, fixing the cuffs of his blazer. The guy dressed like a college professor on a budget, with his garish sports jackets and button-down shirts in hues of lavender and sky blue. His brown leather shoes only added to the dull old man look, though the guy was a couple of years younger than me. His outfits never ceased to hurt my eyes.

I watched him go, taking a long swig of my beer. When he hugged Kandra earlier, she had not been into it, but the douche hadn't read the signals that were clear as day. Benji settled down in a chair beside Miranda, most likely trying to strong-arm her for an interview. She gave him an unreadable glance, but I knew the sheriff could handle herself.

A thought flowed into the edges of my mind. What if Benji asked Kandra for a story? Everyone knew the girl who'd left as a photographer with a dream and wound up becoming a beautiful model living the high life in the fast lane.

I heard rumors that she had gotten engaged to the guy who was her agent. It wasn't a scandal, but it rubbed me the wrong way. Not because I gave a damn that she got engaged, but because her agent should have been impartial. It was his job to protect her and look after her best interests. He had power over her entire career and shouldn't have been emotionally or physically involved with her.

Why am I thinking about this? Kandra, her agent, her engagement, or whatever happened between them, meant absolutely nothing to me. And I certainly didn't care about her and Benji. She wasn't my woman, and I sure as hell wasn't going to come between her and anyone else in her life. She might be back, but we weren't back to the people we were before she left.

I took another drink and noticed Miranda get out of her seat and head for the door. She and Roy eyed each other, and he gave her a slight nod. She scanned my table, and I'd swear there was a hint of disappointment in her expression before she left Benji sitting there alone and talking at her retreating back.

"Here you go." Kandra approached and placed the steaming garlic knots before me and exhaled.

I stared at her, confused. Was she holding her breath?

"Enjoy." She turned to go, but I grabbed her wrist without thinking. The second my skin met hers, something crackled between us like a static charge before a lightning strike. I let her go as if she burned me, but she turned to face me with wide eyes.

"We need to talk," I said.

Her delicate throat shifted as she swallowed. She looked over her shoulder at Roy, then dropped into the seat beside me.

Across the room, Benji watched us.

"Right now?" Her low voice strained like she was holding back her emotions. The defeated set of her shoulders made me wonder if she knew what I wanted to talk about.

She leveled with me about her need to make the best of things, but I also needed that chance, and it would be easier without her in my path.

"This is my favorite hangout." I sipped my beer, and she blinked, then nodded. Her brows knitted together.

"Makes sense, seeing it's the only bar in town."

"My brothers and I come here almost every day after work." I stared into my glass, refusing to look at her, but I was as aware of her as I'd be an angry bear or a rabid dog.

"That's great." Her cheerful answer didn't match the flat tone of her voice.

"What I need you to do is make sure that someone else takes

our orders. I can ask Roy later." I glanced at her as raw panic filled her eyes, chased by the sheen of tears.

"He'll think I upset you."

Her ragged whisper made me shake my head.

"I'll assure him you didn't. I just think it would be best for the both of us to keep our distance. I don't want either of us to be uncomfortable. You understand, right?"

Relief seeped into her features, but hurt gathered on the rim of her lower lids and threatened to overflow.

She nodded. "Yes. Fine," she said, but her tone implied my solution was everything but fine.

Every man knew that when a girl said fine, it wasn't.

I could have kept her from standing. I could have explained myself—my fears and concerns. I could have told her why, but I didn't stop her as she stood up and stared at me. She gripped the edge of the table like she might collapse. After a deep inhale, she spun around and left me alone to drown my sorrows in beer.

CHAPTER FOUR

KANDRA

Pain chewed at me, and I sucked in a deep, trembling breath as I walked behind the bar.

"Time for your fifteen-minute break." Roy's voice drowned out the words—words circling my brain like ravenous vultures, ready to devour whatever last vestige of self-esteem I had left.

"Thank you." Without giving him a chance to look at my face, I slipped out the back door and into the alleyway. Breathing in the crisp evening air, I walked down the steps and put my back to the brick wall and slid down to the ground, my shirt catching on the rough parts as I made my way to the asphalt. The clean alleyway didn't have a shred of trash, not even a stray cigarette butt. The only thing that shouldn't have been there was the brilliant green moss growing on the edges of the concrete road and maybe ... me.

One of the things I loved about this place was the pride its residents took in the town. Every person had ownership.

When I was younger, Cross Creek seemed like a suffocating place, but as an adult, I understood why my parents thought it was the perfect place to raise a family. It was safe and quiet, and everyone knew each other—everyone cared.

Cross Creek didn't come with big-town problems or attitudes. The people here looked out for one another.

"I didn't think it would be like this." I pulled my legs to my chest and put my forehead on my knees.

"Careful talking to yourself. People might start to think you're crazy." I recognized Gypsy's voice but didn't lift my head.

"Maybe I am crazy." Why had I come back? Sure, the town was a great place, but I knew I'd run into Noah again. Maybe in the furthest reaches of my heart and mind, I hoped we could be friends. Not that we could be together because everything had become so ridiculously complicated, but seeing him again stirred things inside me.

The sound of something scraping the wall beside me was all the proof I needed that Gypsy had sat down next to me. "What makes you think that?" A tender hand patted my shoulder.

"I came back. That's pretty crazy."

"Seems like a smart move to me." Her cheerful tone did nothing to brighten my mood since she didn't know the whole story.

"I thought Noah would have gotten over the anger and pain I caused him." Tears stung my eyes.

"Did you really think that, or did you just hope he'd magically forget?"

I lifted both shoulders, then let them drop.

"Honey, he was gutted when you left. You hurt him because he loved you and he missed you terribly."

Loved—past tense. Somehow that stung more than anything else, but what could I expect? I left and moved on. I made choices that I'd have to live with all my life. "Thanks," I said as kindly as I could while fresh tears clung to my lashes.

Ugh, would I be a mess like this all the time?

"I don't feel like I was helpful," Gypsy said.

"It's not you. It's just ... a mess. All of it." I wasn't about to get into details. I could hardly admit them to myself, much less anyone else.

"I thought he might keep me at arm's length because I hurt him. That is an understandable reaction, but he's downright cold and verging on mean."

"Of course, he'd be guarded. He's afraid you'll hurt him again. I bet he still loves you. I could ask him if you want."

"No!" I grabbed her arm to stop her as she stood up. "Please don't," I begged.

She nodded, her kind eyes sparkling. "Okay, I won't ask him."

I let her go, and she walked toward the door before turning back to me. "You can ask him yourself. I'll send him out." With that, she slipped back inside, and I groaned.

There was no way she would talk him into coming out. Noah could barely look at me, much less exit the bar to speak to me.

Besides, I wasn't sure I could take more of his hostility, no matter how deserved it might be.

The last words he said were still on repeat like a crappy song in my brain. *Roy's is my favorite hangout. My brothers and I come here almost every day after work. What I need you to do is make sure that someone else—anyone else—takes our orders and comes to our table. I'm letting you know first, but I'll tell Roy later.*

The words still smarted. I hung my head, feeling humiliated. Our past was so bad he couldn't even stomach the thought of seeing me. No, it was worse than that. He thought I'd ruin his favorite place.

Not that I had a lot of choices, but maybe I shouldn't have come back.

The door opened, and Noah's tall, muscular frame filled it before moving down the steps toward me. I refused to look him in the eyes, and instead, put my head back down. "Did Gypsy put you up to this?" *How the heck did she talk him into coming out here to speak to me?*

"Yes." His careful, neutral voice didn't betray a hint of what he was thinking, not that I needed to know. I could imagine whatever I wanted about Noah, but the fact that he was here, beside me, had to mean something. Maybe there was hope of a friendship for us, after all.

"Look, I'm sorry for the things I said to you before I left. I burned bridges, and I regret it." I hadn't intended things to sound so bad, but I could close my eyes and still see the hurt in his when he begged me not to go and promised we'd be happy in Cross Creek. I told him I needed more than the town could offer—more than he could offer. Even now, the thought of it made me cringe.

"I'm not the same person I was when I left." A lump the size of a garlic knot stuck in my throat, and it took two swallows to get it down.

"I know. You're a world-famous model, and up until two weeks ago, you were engaged to your agent. The photographer with a dream became the subject in magazines."

I sucked in a deep breath as the razor's edge of pain sliced me open. "You heard about that, huh?"

"How could I not? For a minute, you were news. You were a fresh face with promise and talent, and you threw away everything for an agent who ran you into the ground." His harsh words lanced through me like an arrow to the stomach—a gutshot and not even a clean kill.

"He didn't run me into the ground." *Why was I protecting Anthony?* "I started out taking pictures of models. Then Anthony saw me and told me I should be in front of the camera." Thinking back, he'd been so sweet and sincere, or at least he seemed to be.

Noah snorted. "The guy was a predator. He was threatened by your skill, so he eliminated the competition."

"He was an agent, not a photographer." It was sweet that Noah thought so highly of my photography. "Are you saying you think he lied to me? That I shouldn't have been in front of the camera?" I lifted my head to look at him.

He shook his head. "That's not what I'm saying. Obviously, you're beautiful. You don't need to fish for compliments." His frosty tone chilled me to the bone.

Noah had always supported my dream to be a photographer. I could remember days spent stretched out on my bed, showing him the newest pictures I had taken. He confided that my images made him feel something. Now all he felt around me was anger.

Once, I showed him a picture I'd captured of an intimate family moment of him with his brothers and father laughing, and he said it was his favorite. That image still lived on the SD card in my camera because I never deleted it or several others of him and his family.

"So, how is your family?"

He tensed up and didn't respond at first, and then said, "A lot has changed since you left, and I don't feel like getting into it right now."

"I get it." I tilted my head back and rested it on the wall. "Nothing is working out as I expected. When I left, I thought I had all the answers." I snorted. "Now, I'm pretty sure I didn't know anything."

"Were you happy?"

"I thought I was happy with Anthony—kind of. He was good to me for a while." Not at the end, though. He tossed me aside like moldy bread. "Modeling was fun. It was a new challenge, and a skill I didn't have at first. I had to work my ass off, but I enjoyed it."

Noah sat quietly, but when I glanced at him, I noticed he seemed to be hanging on every word. His ability to listen warmed my heart and perforated it at the same time.

"Sadly, in the modeling industry, a woman is over the hill before she hits thirty. I was lucky to continue getting jobs for as long as I did. When the calls stopped coming in, I didn't mind, because I thought I had Anthony." Fresh tears stung my eyes, and my throat burned like I consumed rolls of sandpaper and chased them down with shots of vodka. "He always said I was charming and talented. He used to call me beautiful like it was my name."

Noah let out a grunting noise that told me exactly what he thought of Anthony.

I continued talking like he hadn't accurately figured out my ex.

"But in the end, it didn't work out." I couldn't articulate what actually happened. Anthony had left me for someone younger, more charming, and far more beautiful. She didn't have an ounce of fat or modeling talent in her whole body. Her only gift was her mouth, and it had nothing to do with her smile.

"Now I'm back in Cross Creek." Sitting in the alley behind Roy's Bar on the ground with the first love of my life made everything come full circle.

I studied the white clouds slowly floating across the darkening sky. Where would they go? Would they move someplace new, or would the blackness devour them and leave nothing behind? "You know, all my best memories here are with you. It's strange coming back to find out you hate me."

"Do you blame me?"

Inside, I heard the shattering of my heart. "No."

We sat in silence for a moment. "Why did you come out here?"

He didn't answer, and I wondered what Gypsy had said to get him to join me.

There was something else that tickled the edge of my mind, and I had to know.

"Roy said if he hadn't stepped in when Benji was talking to me, table eight would have. Do you have a problem with Benji?"

Did he have that same nagging sense of unease with the town columnist?

"I don't care who you choose to see or talk to." Noah's crisp tone didn't give me the backup I hoped for.

We sat in silence for another moment, and then I stood. "My fifteen is probably over. Thank you for listening." My feet throbbed painfully. I was ready for this incredibly difficult first shift to be over so I could go home, run a bath, and cry.

As I walked toward the back door, I looked back at Noah. His eyes locked on mine, and emotions washed over me.

He once loved me, and seeing him again made me realize I never stopped loving him. Once you let someone into your heart, they stayed there forever. Noah would always own a piece of me—the young, innocent, and foolish piece. The heart of a girl who thought everything was butterflies and rainbows. *Silly girl.*

"Have a good night," I said. "Get home safely." I opened the door and let myself back into the bar. Why hadn't I told him the whole truth? Why did I leave out the most crucial part of why Anthony dumped me?

Why hadn't I told Noah that my ex left me when he found out I was pregnant?

CHAPTER FIVE

NOAH

"It's only Wednesday, and you don't get to burn out yet." Quinn clapped a hand on my shoulder.

I watched Miranda walk with Bayden toward one of the work trucks. Yep, there was absolutely something between them. Bayden would never let someone on-site unless they were part of our crew. Allowing Miranda to tour the new police department we were building for Cross Creek was a big deal. He didn't even make her wear a hard hat.

A rogue week-long rain had slowed our timeline down. We couldn't pour concrete in the deluge, and we were working double-time to get back on track.

Ethan didn't like not being on schedule, and the rest of the crew seemed short on patience. Moods were sour, and the men weren't at their best, and there was Bayden, escorting the sheriff around, anyway.

I shoved Quinn's hand away.

"Leave me be and let me wallow in my misery."

"You can't be miserable. You've got one amazing brother." He pointed to himself. "And you were part of the crew that built the

Guild Creative Center in Aspen Cove." Quinn's infectious smile lit up his face. "What could you possibly be so sullen about?"

"That was a sweet build." I thought about Aspen Cove and wondered if it was time to move. The town was charming, and there was no Kandra at Bishop's Brewhouse.

I turned away, but Quinn fell into step beside me.

"It's about *her*, isn't it? Kandra?"

Without a word, I pulled open the bathroom door. Quinn backed off a step, and I walked inside, locking the door behind me. I could only hope he'd get the hint to leave.

"Did you take her home?" he yelled through the door.

That was loud enough for everyone to hear. I opened the door and grabbed his collar, yanking him off-balance. "I'm done talking about this, and so are you," I snarled.

Shoving him back, I closed and locked the door once more.

"I knew there was something there. Way to go, brother." His voice faded as if he was walking away, and I squeezed my eyes closed. If he didn't lay off, I would choke him to death.

Behind my closed lids, her face took residence. Those blue eyes blinked, and her lips curved into a hesitant smile. *You know, all my best memories are here with you. It's strange coming back to find out that you hate me.*

I still remember her telling me ten years ago that I couldn't provide the life she wanted. I never thought she was the type of woman that would gut me with her words and walk away while I bled. I never thought she would quit on me until it happened. Yeah, I was in pain, but I didn't hate her. I felt angry and betrayed, but I could never hate her because I loved her.

Nothing is working out as I expected. When I left, I thought I had all the answers.

Our conversation the day she tore my heart in two had been her telling me what she wanted in life. Were those the answers she'd thought she had that she was no longer sure of? Was she coyly trying to tell me she wanted another go at us? I rolled my eyes. That would never happen.

I'm not the same person I was when I left.

She was right about that. I couldn't pinpoint exactly what changed, but something about her had because she was different. Just as pretty, but wounded in some way. The light in her eyes had dimmed. Her confidence was gone. Kandra Sullivan had left an inferno and came back a puff of smoke. All the spark in her personality was gone, or was it merely waiting for the right moment to ignite?

Why had she asked me if I had a problem with Benji? Was she fishing to see if I was jealous, just like she'd done when she wanted me to say she was beautiful?

Someone pounded on the door, and I pulled it open, looking around for Quinn, but he was nowhere in sight. Ryan, a member of the crew, walked inside.

I walked out and thought about Kandra and our conversation some more.

When the calls stopped coming in, I didn't mind because I thought I had Anthony.

Anthony ... the guy was a dick. A Harvey Weinstein of the modeling world who probably had a casting couch in every room of his office. He talked her out of taking photographs and instead being in them so he could control her career. He dumped her, and I was sure the jackass knew the hit to her self-esteem would send her running home. If he didn't, then he never really knew Kandra.

Quinn's arm slipped around my shoulders. "How did it go last night?"

I shrugged him off, but Ethan stepped up to my right, pinning me between them. "Still single? Are we able to go to the bar, or did you get us booted?"

"Did you kill anyone or smash any faces?" Bayden's voice

chimed in from behind, and when I swung around to face him, Miranda studied me with suspicion.

"He's kidding." I didn't need the sheriff looking at me like I had something to hide. "Nobody got killed or maimed. It was all very civil." I stepped onto the dirt, heading back to work, but my brothers stood still. "Don't you have work to do?" I asked as I pivoted to face them.

Quinn shrugged. "Fifteen-minute break?"

"Aren't you going to tell us what happened?" Ethan crossed his arms the way our dad did when he was waiting for an answer, and I wanted to deck him.

"She told me what happened since she left, and then she went back to work, and I went home." It had all been so innocent, but I doubted my brothers would believe me. "I'm done talking about it, so stop asking."

"He's sensitive, which means something happened." Quinn rubbed his hands together while his eyes sparkled with mischief.

"Nothing happened." And nothing would happen because I had to be on guard with her. I realized something last night; despite her being gone all those years, nothing had changed; Kandra still had my heart. She managed to make me feel something, and it didn't matter that those emotions were anger and betrayal.

All the pseudo-relationships I'd been in since her were so topical I'd never felt any loss or sadness when they ended. Maybe that was because I never let anyone in after her. Somehow, her coming back to Cross Creek made it feel like she never left. That hole in my heart was now plugged, even though the pain seeped through.

I sounded stupid and sappy and sentimental. Kandra coming back didn't change anything that happened before. She had left me because I wasn't enough, and it broke me.

"I was right, you're still in love with her." Quinn's glee and my dark inner thoughts clashed.

"Did you forget what today is?" I grumbled, leaning in closer to him. Today was not a day for him to push me, to joke around, or to be so playful. It should be a somber day of silence and respect.

Quinn's eyes narrowed, and his brows furrowed. "I know what today is." His voice was razor-sharp.

"Do you? If so, then where's your respect?"

"You know me better than that, and I don't think Dad would want us to be sad and mopey." Quinn's quiet anger snapped in his voice.

I was tired of the fun and games on such a mournful day. My relationship with other ghosts of the past didn't matter today. "Why do you always act like nothing happened?" I stepped closer to Quinn, who stood his ground and studied me calmly.

"You grieve your way, and I'll grieve mine." His even tone did nothing to calm the anger eating at the lining of my gut.

"Do you grieve, or is life all a joke to you?" I watched his pupils dilate. "You're so focused on me and some woman that walked out of my life a decade ago instead of the fact that today is the second anniversary of our father's death."

Quinn's Adam's apple bobbed.

"Look, even if there was something between us—and there isn't—today is not the day, okay?" I stepped around him and headed for my truck. My chest caved in like a wrecking ball had crashed into my sternum.

I sat in the cab, holding back the pain, when someone rapped on the glass. The sharp sound, like point-blank gunshots, invaded my skull.

I glanced out at Max, the mail carrier.

He motioned for me to roll down the window, and I did, because next to my father, he was the best man I knew, and the closest thing to a father figure I had left. "This is for you." He dug an envelope out of his bag while running his other hand through his hair. It had stayed dark despite his age but was going salt and pepper at the temples. Unlike his hair, his close-clipped beard and goatee were mostly gray with a few black hairs.

"You're delivering mail to my truck now? They better be bumping your pay grade."

Max chuckled. "It's actually from me to you. I know this is a difficult day." His dark eyes met mine.

I inhaled and took the envelope he offered. Tapping it against the steering wheel, I considered whether or not to say something.

"I blew up at Quinn today. He's just so … cavalier. Today is supposed to be a day of somber respect." I trusted that whatever I told Max stayed with him, unlike Dottie, the diner owner, who would gossip her way to the pearly gates. Max was a good man.

"You're upset. Quinn is likely wounded too, but you're both individuals, so it stands to reason you'd handle loss and pain differently. It's hard to understand, but I know he doesn't mean any harm."

"Should I apologize?"

He snorted. "Probably not; it's Quinn, and there's no doubt he deserves your ire for something or another."

I chuckled while staring at the sealed envelope that had nothing written on the front. "Thank you for this," I said, holding it up.

"You haven't opened it yet, so why are you thanking me?"

"I feel like I should wait to open it until I need to, if that makes any sense."

He nodded. "It makes perfect sense." He shifted his weight as if getting ready to walk away but hesitated. Sucking in a deep breath, he glanced at me. "You know, Kandra is a good woman. She's not perfect, but nobody is, and if she makes you happy, you should let go of the past and go for it."

I didn't need to ask how he knew, because there were no

secrets in a small town. Even so, I knew I could always trust him to keep mine.

"It's not that simple." I rubbed my chin, feeling the start of a rough shadow against my palm. "She broke my heart, Max, and I won't give her the chance to do it again."

"Because you're sure she'll let you down, or because you're afraid she won't?"

I considered his words, and he was right. I was equally afraid of both outcomes. I didn't know if I was ready to settle down now, but if I were, Kandra had always been the woman I imagined beside me.

"You two were just kids. Not saying the love wasn't real, but you've had ten years to grow up. Ten years to understand what you want and need. You were always an old soul, Noah, much older than your years, but she may have needed time to grow. She's a sweet one and mark my words, someone will win her heart. The question is, will you forgive yourself if you don't try again?" Max lowered his head to dig inside his bag again, giving me a moment with my thoughts.

The idea of her finding someone else sent white-hot anger flashing through me.

It was ridiculous to feel jealous because she wasn't mine. Even though I'd once been hers, maybe she never ever truly belonged to me.

Still, she wasn't the same person she'd been when she left. Life had knocked her down a peg, but instead of letting it break her, she held her head high. I had to give her that, Kandra was a willow and while she might bend, she wouldn't break.

Her words ran through my head.

This is my life, and I'm trying to make the best of it.

"Is it worth getting hurt again?" I honestly didn't know. It sounded stupid and cliché, but it was the truth. Losing her was like losing a limb. I hadn't been whole after she left. That was something I hadn't revealed to anyone.

Max lifted both shoulders, his eyes locking on mine once more. "I can't answer that for you. Maybe you have to let your heart decide."

CHAPTER SIX

KANDRA

I wiped my mouth with the back of my trembling hand. Nausea turned my stomach, and I silently begged my body not to throw up again.

Turning on the sink, I splashed cold water on my face and rubbed my hands over my stinging skin. I hated vomiting. It was about the worst feeling in the whole world. My nose burned, my eyes watered, and my throat was so raw no amount of honey could soothe it. To make things worse, I shook like an alcoholic at rehab.

Meeting my tired gaze in the bathroom mirror, I exhaled slowly. The girl staring back at me looked scared with her wide eyes, darkened with delicate smudges that made her look like she hadn't slept a decent night in months.

Last night, I got off work at two after Roy approved a couple of overtime hours so I could help him close. He walked me to my car and waited until I drove off before going to his truck. It was sweet, but there was no crime to speak of in Cross Creek unless you counted the local teens knocking down mailboxes. Or Mrs. Barry stealing someone's Sunday newspaper for the coupons.

I felt safe from nefarious activity, but I appreciated the gesture.

For a boss, Roy was shaping up to be a good one which made me feel awful for not telling him the truth. I clung to the edges of the sink until my fingers ached. I was keeping this pregnancy under wraps, but why?

Wouldn't it be easier to tell people now? I mean, what would I do when Roy asked me to carry something heavy? It was part of the job I agreed to do when he hired me.

With viscous questions circling like sharks and no answers coming, I turned off the water, patted my face with a towel, and left the room.

A glance at the clock on my bedside table told me it was nearly noon. Sheesh, the whole day was slipping by, and all I'd accomplished was puking my guts up and realizing I had too many questions and no real answers. My belly turned, and I dropped on the edge of my bed. My hands wouldn't stop trembling as I ran my fingers through my hair, twisting it up into a messy bun I could fix later. I prayed I wouldn't start heaving again.

Thankfully, I didn't have to work until four. With any luck, Roy would let me have the extra two hours of overtime again to help him close. I needed the money because life would get a lot more expensive, very soon.

I doubted I could count on Anthony for child support. He wanted no part of having a baby. And unless I wanted to sue him, I was on my own. People who didn't have money couldn't win against those who did, and Anthony was loaded.

I stood up and yawned as the world went black behind my eyes and waited for the lightheaded feeling to pass. Everything came back into focus, and I exhaled.

As I got dressed, I wondered when I'd stop being able to button my jeans. How long would I even be able to keep my secret?

A movement outside my window caught my eye, and I hurried out the front door. The bright sunshine assaulted me, and I shaded my face with one hand as I rushed to the mailbox.

"Max!" I remembered the old mail carrier. He'd always been kind and gave the best advice when I needed him. There was no way I'd let him move past my place without a proper hello.

His face lit up, and when he opened his arms, I rushed into the hug. "You're back," he said.

I stepped away and gave him a look. "You already knew that, so don't try to pretend." Nothing got past the mailman; outside of the local police, Dottie, and Roy, he knew the most about the locals.

With a slight smile, he loaded my mailbox. "You're right, I did. This is from me to you." He held out a white envelope, and I reached for it, but he pulled it back. "Too slow!"

I laughed. When I was a little girl, we played this game, and the memory of the times when he stopped and chatted with my parents and slipped me a piece of candy or a new book, filled me with warmth. Max always felt like part of the family.

He touched the envelope to my hand, and I took it. The blank white paper gave no hint to what was inside, and I turned it over. The flap was tucked into the envelope, but it wasn't sealed.

"Thank you." I smiled at him.

"You don't even know what it is." His jeering brought a smile to my lips, and I shifted back and forth on my feet. "Aren't you going to open it?"

"I'm a bit emotional these days and should probably be alone when I do, but thank you for thinking of me." I opened my mailbox, and he turned as if to leave, but hesitated for a moment and twisted to face me once more. A thoughtful look softened his face.

"You know, you're glowing."

I sucked in a deep breath. Of course, he knew. There were no secrets from Max; somehow, I'd given myself away. Hopefully, he was the only one who had figured it out.

"I'm not telling anyone yet," I whispered the words. "I mean, I'm not that far along, and until I hit that safe mark, it doesn't make sense to share."

He dipped his head and lifted a hand. "I can respect that, but is that the real reason?"

He always had a way of seeing right through me. "It's complicated." It wasn't all that complicated. I had failed. I left everything I loved, hoping for something better, and I ended up with less. I hadn't even told my mother. I could still hear the words she told me the day I left. *"You are capable of anything you set your mind to. Conquer the world."* She hugged me and then whispered in my ear. *"For God's sake, don't let anyone take advantage of you, and don't get knocked up. There's nothing like a child to change the trajectory of your life. You were born for great things."* Won't Mom be proud of me now?

"I appreciate your discretion."

Max looked up at me with compassionate eyes, "Of course, it's not my story to tell."

Relief hit me like a freight train, and my shoulders dropped a little. It was Max, and of all people, I knew he would keep my secret safe.

"With that out of the way, let me be the first to say congratulations." His hand wrapped around mine and his warm fingers gently squeezed.

"I haven't even told my mother," I said.

He sighed and rolled his eyes heavenward. "I know because if your mother knew you were pregnant, she would have told the whole town. I'm likely the first to know, or darn close to it."

"You're quite the Sherlock Holmes, huh?" I couldn't hold back a laugh. Max was easily the smartest person I'd ever met. Thankfully, he was also a good guy who used his powers to help people instead of hurting them.

"Nah, chasing bad guys isn't my style." He chuckled, patted my hand, and let me go. "Do you want to talk about it? Secrets are heavy, and they come with a price that's hard to pay alone."

His words shot through my heart, and instant tears stung my eyes. He was right about all of it. "I thought he loved me." The words left my mouth in a whisper, and I glanced up, trying to hold back my tears. So many times, I wanted to pick up the phone to call my best friend Melanie, but I wasn't ready for advice. Friends and mothers couldn't help themselves; they wanted to try to fix things, but Max ... he would just listen, and I needed his ears.

"Oh, sweetie." He pulled me in for another hug, and I held on this time. Grateful for the comfort, I squeezed my eyes closed and let it all slip out.

"The second he found out I was pregnant, he moved on with another woman." A beautiful woman who was younger and the next big thing. *Was Noah right? Had Anthony been a predator all along?* The more I thought about it, the more uneasy I felt.

Max pulled back and smiled down at me. It was a grin so big I could see every tooth in his mouth and couldn't hold back the slight tug at the corners of my lips. I wiped away my embarrassing tears. Gosh, I was such a mess lately.

"It's his loss, and he'll have no idea how big that will be until it's too late to fix."

"There's no fixing this." I patted my stomach. "Is it wrong that I'm not telling anyone?"

He shifted, touching his chin with one hand. "It depends on why you aren't telling anyone."

I lowered my head and stared at the pavement beneath my feet. Sighing, I tried to keep my voice even and calm, though it wobbled at the edges. "I'm ashamed. Ashamed that he left me knowing I was pregnant and that I'm going to be a single mom.

Ashamed that I didn't have what it took to keep him interested. I believed he loved me, so mostly I'm ashamed of my ignorance." There was no way he could have loved me but then dump me once he found out I was having his baby. Worse yet, he moved on within minutes. Minutes! I meant nothing to him. I was just another pretty face in a whole line of beautiful faces. I should have known better.

"There's no need to be ashamed. This is the twenty-first century." His kind smile lifted my spirits. "I'm pretty sure it's in style nowadays to be a single mom. I saw a show about it on TV."

Not exactly the yardstick I wanted to measure my life by, but I appreciated his perspective. He was right though; the stigma of being a single mom was not as bad as it had been in the past.

"I had everything, and I lost it," I whispered. It felt good to be honest and open up to someone. I rubbed my stomach. "But I'm actually kind of excited."

"I'm glad. What excites you the most?" He leaned against my mailbox and planted an elbow on top while focusing on me like I was the only person in the world.

I couldn't hold back a smile. "I'm excited to be a mom. Even though I'm afraid to do it alone, I'm looking forward to the experience. I may have failed in my life, but I won't fail him or her."

"You're strong and capable, and you'll be a wonderful mom." He patted my shoulder. "I'm glad you're home."

I nodded. "I'm happy to be here." Noah's face filled my mind. Our conversation echoed in my brain, and I sucked in a sharp breath. *You know, all my best memories are here with you. It's strange coming back to find out that you hate me.* I could see the glacial chill in his eyes as he responded. *Do you blame me?* "Well, mostly happy, at least."

"Uh-oh, that doesn't sound positive." Max crossed his arms and widened his stance as a light breeze kicked up. "What happened?"

I touched my hair, remembering I'd just put it up quickly, and I must look a mess. "Well, Noah hates me."

Max snorted. "He doesn't hate you. The man's still in love with you. You just need him to pull his head out of his backside and figure it out."

Stunned, I stared at Max. "But ... he said he hated me."

Max's brows shot up far enough to hide under his sweep of bangs. "He told you he hated you?"

I fidgeted with the hem of my shirt, tugging at a loose thread. "Not exactly. I said it was strange to come back to him hating me, and he asked if I blamed him." I peered up and watched his expression go slack for a moment, then snap into a smile.

"See, he doesn't hate you." He waggled a finger at me. "He was just probing to see if you thought he had a right to hate you. That's not the same thing."

I blinked. "Not everyone will like me, and I can live with that, but he *does* have a reason to hate me." I cleared my throat, trying to get the bitter taste that sat in the back to go away.

"I know your split back in the day wasn't easy, but you're not that young woman anymore, and he's not the same young man." Max's knowing smile made me wonder what he wasn't sharing.

"You're right."

"I know." He laughed out loud, the sound of his deep rumble ringing off the pavement. The trees shifted in the breeze, and the movement and sunlight made shadows dance on the green grass. A car drove past on the quiet street, and we both waved because that was expected in a small town.

Max gave me a serious expression. "Obviously, that guy wasn't the right one." He nodded at my belly, and I crossed my arms protectively under my ribs.

"Nope, you're right."

"Maybe now that you're home, you can find the right one. Who knows," he said, tilting his head, "maybe you already have."

"Well, you're fantastic, Max, you really are, but you're married and a bit old for me."

He threw his head back and laughed before saying, "I wasn't talking about me."

I knew Max thought the right man was Noah, and I couldn't help but wish it were true.

CHAPTER SEVEN

NOAH

"I'm freaking starving, and I hate Mondays." Quinn gave a hangry shake of his head while Ethan stared at him.

"What does Monday have to do with you being hungry?" Ethan's suspicious tone seemed to offend Quinn, and when I groaned, both my brothers looked at me.

"Now you're engaging in the conversation because he's complaining?"

I glanced toward Bayden's truck and saw he wasn't in it. I hadn't seen him out and about among the crew working either.

Quinn crossed his arms and narrowed his eyes, scanning the area. He, too, must have been looking for Bayden. It was unlike our brother to pull a disappearing act without telling anyone where he went.

"It's Monday, and Mondays always suck. Only bad things happen on this day," Quinn complained.

"No, they don't, why would you say that?" I thought about losing Dad and about Kandra breaking my heart. Then my thoughts went to Kandra coming back. None of those things happened on a Monday.

Quinn sighed, but before he could answer, out of nowhere, Bayden walked past us.

"I forgot my lunch." His angry tone was unmistakable, and Quinn's arms broke out of their crossed position as he swept his right hand at his twin's receding form. "See, it's because it's Monday."

Ethan shook his head, and I turned to walk away. Might as well see what had Bayden all twisted up.

Quinn might be the glue that held this brotherhood together, but he would sabotage a situation just to prove that Mondays were evil.

I sped to a light jog to catch up with Bayden. "Yo, what's up?"

He turned to look at me, and his expression was as dark as thunderclouds. "Nothing's up."

Coming to a halt in front of him, I lifted both hands in a gesture of defeat. "I'm not going to pry." If he didn't want to talk about it, I wouldn't push. "But I'm here if you need to talk, okay? Things are rough right now. I get it."

He shrugged my hand off and looked to his right. "No, you don't, but thanks." Without another word, he left.

Quinn rushed forward, stopping at my side. "What did you say to him?" He shielded the sun from his eyes with one hand and stared after Bayden.

"Nothing." I turned to leave. Someone had to work while we were on-site, and it sure as hell wouldn't be Quinn because he hated Mondays.

"Bayden!" Quinn shouted through cupped hands.

I kept walking.

"Creekside Diner for lunch. I'll buy yours," he yelled. "We don't want to starve to death."

I glanced back in time to see Bayden flip him the bird before storming into the bathroom.

I chuckled. Yep, those were my brothers.

A moment later, the sound of quickly approaching footsteps warned me that Quinn was coming in fast.

"Touch me, and I'll drop you," I growled.

"Don't worry; I don't want to touch you." He clapped a hand on my shoulder.

I stared at it, then gave him a look that I hoped said *drop it or die*. His hand fell away, and he wiped it on his thighs. "Right. I'm not sure if you heard, but we're doing lunch at Creekside. I'll let Ethan know."

Creekside was the last place on my list to visit. At the diner, we'd run into Dottie. My only hope was that she wouldn't chew me up and spit me out.

WE'D BARELY MADE it in the door when we heard, "Boys!" Dottie pulled Quinn and Bayden in for hugs. Quinn wound an arm around her shoulder, leaned in, and gave a gentle squeeze, while Bayden stood stiff and uncomfortable. The twins couldn't be more different at that moment. Quinn seemed at ease, and in his element, while Bayden acted like he'd rather burst into flames than spend another moment in that embrace.

Dottie let them go and tried to hook an arm around Ethan and me. I gracefully accepted the hug, while Ethan ducked, his attention locked on his phone, as usual.

"Hi Dottie," I said, glaring at Ethan.

Quinn elbowed him, and he glanced at our brother, then at me before mouthing, *what?*

I narrowed my eyes. Playing innocent wasn't going to fly. Our parents taught us better than that. What would it have cost him to hug the older woman?

"You boys never come in for lunch. Must be a special day."

Dottie followed my brothers to their favorite table. I sat next to Ethan to elbow him in the ribs. He inched away from me.

Quinn looked up at Dottie. "Yes, ma'am. Bayden forgot his lunch at home, so I'm going to play momma and feed the poor boy. You know he's a growing lad and needs square meals to keep up his strength." By Quinn's grunt, I knew he'd earned a sharp blow from Bayden's steel-toed boot.

The twins glared one another down, and I saw the thought process working through their brains. They were deciding if their difference of opinion was worth a full-blown fistfight in front of Dottie. She would drag them out by their ears if they dared, and it wouldn't be the first time she'd done it, either.

They seemed to cool it, and Quinn smiled at her. "You're looking lovely today."

"You stop that." She waved him off. Her white hair was gathered back in a bun, and fine lines and wrinkles took over her face, but under the signs of aging was a bone structure that had to have been beautiful once. On the flip side of delicate beauty was a fiery spirit. The woman might be a terrible gossip, but she wouldn't take shit from anyone.

Quinn flashed a grin that told me he was testing her. "I'd like the ribs."

Oh great, the barbecue sauce would be everywhere once he got back to work. The man ate like an animal.

She wrote it down before scanning the rest of us.

"I'll have the pancakes, please," I said.

"Second that," Bayden added.

Ethan lifted a hand slightly without ever taking his eyes off his phone. "Pancakes, too, please, and thank you."

She nodded, her lips moving as if she were reciting the order as she wrote it all down. After she left, Quinn snatched Ethan's phone and tried to pass it to me as our brother lunged after it. I caught the phone and slipped it under the table, giving it to Bayden while Ethan glowered.

"Since when are you on his side?" he asked, his tone incredulous.

"Since you sidestepped that hug and made me take the brunt of it." I showed him my hands to prove I didn't have his phone. "Besides, you can join us for one meal. Just one, and then you can have your phone back."

"Yeah, what are you doing on here, anyway?" Quinn glanced under the table and grinned.

He quietly handed the phone back, cleared his throat, and said, "Carry on."

"What did you see?" Bayden asked. His whole body still except for his eyes, which slid back and forth between Quinn and Ethan.

"Nothing." Quinn cleared his throat. "Okay, he was on RedTube, but hey if he wants to watch Mexican donkey sex that's fine with me."

Ethan turned his phone off and pushed it to the center of the table. "You're such a dick."

"Seriously? He was watching that?" Bayden asked, slumping back in his seat as Dottie walked over with waters. She placed one before each of us, and like the mannered men we were raised to be, we thanked her.

I waited to see how this would play out, but Ethan scowled at Quinn, and Quinn didn't say any more.

"Did you know Kandra is back?" Dottie asked, and I groaned internally.

"You don't say?" Quinn's gaze slid to me, making me want to kick him under the table.

Dottie nodded. "She is, and the whole town is abuzz about it."

"You hear that, Noah? Kandra is back." Quinn stared me down while I held back the urge to give him the finger.

The door opened, and I breathed a sigh of relief as Max stepped inside. "I'll be right back," I stood up and made my way to Max, who stopped and smiled when he saw me.

"Hi," I said with enthusiasm, happy to escape the conversation at my table.

He leaned over and glanced behind me, then straightened up and focused on me again. "Your brothers giving you trouble?"

"Always."

He leaned against the counter and studied me. "Did you open the envelope?"

I shook my head. "Yesterday calmed down a lot for me, and I got through it."

"I didn't have any doubts." He crossed his arms, and I pulled the envelope from my pocket. His eyes widened, and a smile crossed his lips.

I turned it over and tucked my finger under the unsealed flap. I opened it gently and pulled out the card. The front had a beautiful sunset image on it and no words. When I opened it, a receipt fluttered out, and I caught it before it hit the ground. It was a gift that was good for a private ride on Bailee's Farm. All at once, memories crashed over me.

"*I want to be a cowboy!*" *I raced through the house, and Dad gave me a warm smile.*

"*Well, every cowboy needs to learn to rope, herd cattle, and ride a horse,*" *he said.*

I leaped on the couch beside him, my skinny legs dangling off the edge. "*I want to do all those things,*" *I said in a serious voice.*

Dad's eyes twinkled. "*I know just the place. Bailee's farm. He can teach you everything you need to know to be a respectable cowboy.*"

I blinked back the memory and focused on Max again. "Thank you." I couldn't find the words to tell him how perfect the gift was.

By giving me this, he gave me back a piece of my father, and a memory long forgotten.

"You're welcome. I recall how much he believed in you and your dreams." Max's grin grew. "All of them."

He was right. Dad always believed in me, even when I was a stupid kid with impossible dreams.

I opened the card again and read the simple handwritten words on the blank white background.

From Max

Another laugh burst forth. Max could say all the right words at precisely the right moment, but putting sentimental expressions on paper? That wasn't his superpower. Still, the gesture touched me.

"Thank you," I said.

"Food," Quinn called from the table.

Max shook his head and put the mail on the counter. "I think your lunch has arrived," he said, nodding toward the table.

As I headed back to my brothers, the door opened, and the jingling bells hanging to warn Dottie when people came in sounded. I glanced over my shoulder, and my heart took off in a gallop. Nope, that wasn't right; it was a full-on sprint.

Kandra stood there, side by side, next to Benji.

I dropped into my seat, putting my head down, praying she wouldn't notice me. Jealousy churned in my gut, and I tried to shove the feeling away. I had no right to feel resentful because she was here with him. Sure, the guy was a swamp monster, but she had the right to be with whoever she wanted. Hell, maybe she liked vulturous types since that's all she seemed to find after me—first Anthony, and now Benji.

I shook my head.

"Are we hiding?" Quinn asked in a whisper, ducking his head to stare at me.

"Shut up." I was angry that everyone noticed my reaction to

her arrival. I had no right to feel anything about her because she wasn't mine and the sooner I could get that through my thick skull, the better.

"Who are we hiding from?" Quinn glanced over his shoulder. "Benji or Kandra?"

"Piss off, Quinn." I booted him under the table.

"Ow." He tried to kick back but missed. "I know," he said, lighting up like he had a great idea. "We could ask them to join us. I mean, we have plenty of room." He scooted over, squishing an unsuspecting Bayden into the wall. The twins scuffled for a second, and Bayden landed a solid elbow to Quinn's ribs, knocking the wind out of him.

"Don't you dare," I grumbled.

Quinn's eyes danced with mischief as he rubbed his sore side.

CHAPTER EIGHT

KANDRA

"It's just..." Benji let out an exasperated sigh. "I never imagined you working in a bar." He said the word bar with enough disgust that I was insulted for Roy.

"The place is respectable." I picked a table for two to make sure he had no choice but to sit opposite me. Something told me if he had the option to sit next to me and be close, he'd jump at the opportunity. "You go there, so what's the problem?"

His shoulders drooped under his salmon-colored button-down. The tawny sports jacket he wore over it did nothing to mute the loud fashion choice. The disappointment in his features lent him an almost comical air, like an angry cartoon character.

I tried to push aside my rude thoughts as I stared at him. Planting both elbows on the table, he pressed his palms together, brought his hands up to his face, and rested his lips against them. "It's the only place to grab a drink, but it's still a bar."

I sighed. "Okay, what are you concerned about, exactly? Roy walks me to my car at night."

I went quiet as Dottie approached because the woman couldn't keep quiet to save her life, and part of me was terrified that I'd give away my big secret somehow. If she found out now, the whole town would know yesterday. Dottie gossip wasn't constrained to time and space rules.

She stopped at our table. "Kandra. It's so good to see you again, sweetheart. I was just telling people you were back in town."

I didn't doubt that for a second. Everyone in town probably knew my address as well as the number of panties I had in my top drawer. "I'm happy to be back. It's good to see you, Dottie."

She beamed at me as her attention slid to Benji. Her smile pressed thin, then returned to full force as she lifted her pad. "What can I get you, kids?"

"Water." Since I had to watch my caffeine intake and I'd already had coffee today, my choices were limited. I also wanted to keep this visit short and sweet and having a no-cost option allowed me to leave when it was convenient.

My stomach twisted, and I wasn't sure if it was from morning sickness creeping into the afternoon, or nerves.

I wished I hadn't come, but it would have been rude to say no to Benji's invite. Benji wasn't someone you wanted to upset. When he put pen to paper, he could be downright deadly.

Benji looked up at Dottie. "I'd like pancakes for lunch, and she'll have some too." He lifted his chin in my direction before glancing at me. "My treat."

"You and half the restaurant. Must be a Monday thing," Dottie said.

It was a nice gesture, but something about the whole situation, the look in his eyes, the way he said it, everything about the moment rubbed me wrong.

"No, thank you. I had a late breakfast, and I couldn't possibly eat another bite." I patted my belly like I was full, then mentally kicked myself for drawing attention to that area of my body. I wasn't showing, not yet, but I didn't want anyone to have any suspicion about my condition.

Benji's eyes narrowed at me, but he smiled when he looked at Dottie. "Just one, I guess. Thanks, Dottie." He handed her his menu, and the full weight of his attention shifted back to me. The intensity of his stare put me on edge. I sipped the water Dottie dropped off. Curbing the urge to chew the ice chips almost overwhelmed me. I inhaled a deep breath through my nose and continued. "But, back to the conversation before, I'm happy working at Roy's." I met his serious gaze and shifted uncomfortably. Why was he looking at me like he was trying to figure out every thought in my head? "And Roy is a great boss."

"But it's a bar."

I tried my best to hold back my scoff. "Yeah, you've mentioned that. But I still don't see why it's a problem. This is the twenty-first century, and women can have jobs, even in bars." My humor didn't seem to move him, so I took another sip of water. The back of my neck prickled, and I ran a hand over the spot.

"You were a model. Isn't working at a bar a steep fall for you?"

"I was working as a model, and now I am working at a bar. It isn't down, it's parallel. I'm still serving the public, but in a different way." I focused on him instead of the prickling sensation and the rising anger that made my skin tingle.

"I have a proposition." He cleared his throat.

He had a proposition? For me? With a sigh, I said, "Let's hear it."

"You should come work with me." His gaze slipped away, then came back to meet mine.

Stunned, I opened my mouth to respond, but no words came out. I smiled, trying to think of something to say—anything. "At the Sentinel? I'm not a writer." Why would he think I could do the job?

As if I hadn't said a word, he leaned in and lowered his voice. "I have it on good authority that you take beautiful pictures, and you're a career model—both of which are helpful to the paper." He sat back with a pleased look on his face.

Something skittered up my spine like a snake climbing a tree. "Why are you so worried about me and where I work?" There was something weird going on here. Why was he suddenly so concerned about things he shouldn't even care about?

"Because we're friends, and I worry about you." His eyes slid from me, and he thanked Dottie for the coffee as she filled his mug. He added half and half and a generous amount of sugar before stirring. The whole time, I stared at him, unsure what to make of the awkward situation.

"We were friends over a decade ago in high school—and only kind of." I crossed my arms and sat back, determined to get to the bottom of his recent interest in my life. "We were more acquaintances, the kind who said hi to each other in the halls; that hardly counted as *friends*."

He shifted in his seat and peered at something beyond me. "We also took swimming lessons together."

"Benji," I cleared my throat so the words would have a straight path out. "We didn't even run in the same circles." In truth, we weren't that good of friends. I was kind to him because people didn't seem to like him. I wasn't going to be cruel to him or anyone else, but I couldn't help but wonder if he'd taken my kindness to mean something more. "We didn't even hang out."

He let out a rude snort. "Well, how could we? You always had Noah around."

He was right, Noah and I had been inseparable since we'd fallen for one another, but that wasn't why he and I weren't close. "Noah isn't the reason we weren't friends." I said the words slowly, trying to justify my answer.

"Then, why?" Benji asked.

"Why weren't you and I close?" The feeling that I needed to be very careful how I answered washed over me. I thought about guys like him—like Anthony—who I had to tiptoe around to make sure they didn't make my life difficult. Suddenly, I didn't want to spare his feelings anymore.

"If you mean close *close*, as in why we weren't involved, then it's because you're not my type. You weren't then, and you aren't now. You seem like a nice guy, but there will never be anything between us. We don't have chemistry." Saying those words was the most freeing feeling I'd ever experienced. Had I ever told a man how I really felt, or had I always been polite to a fault out of fear that he would take it personally and get mad?

"It's not like that," he said quickly. "I'm just worried about your safety and well-being."

The words didn't ring true, and the feral look in his eyes made me doubt him even more.

"I appreciate that, but I'm safe, and I'm cautious. I'm not stupid or overconfident." I wouldn't risk anything when there was another life at stake other than mine.

"Here you go." Dottie placed a massive plate of pancakes in front of Benji and gave him a blank smile before turning to me. "Do you need anything? Coffee? More water? Something stronger?"

"You don't serve alcohol here," I said with a laugh.

She winked. "I'm sure I could find something if you need it. Just don't tell my boss."

I giggled because she owned the place, so she was the boss, but it was cute.

Obviously, Benji and I were putting out weird vibes, and she picked up on it. There was no doubt the whole town would know that we'd had an awkward lunch. "Thanks, Dottie, I'd love more water."

She reached for my glass, and I pulled it back an inch. "Just water. I was teasing about the other."

She nodded and left.

I focused on Benji, wondering what to do about him. I knew he wasn't telling me the whole truth, but what could I do about it? His insistence that I join him for lunch was weird enough, but this was getting crazy.

While Benji cut into his stack of pancakes, I studied him.

He blinked, his fork going still for a moment. "What?"

I shook my head. "Just thinking."

He stabbed the fork through the fluffy pancakes and drowned the bite in a puddle of syrup. "You're staring."

"You're not telling me everything." I took another sip of water. "I'm trying to figure out why you're holding back." Lowering the glass to the table, I ran my thumb under a drop of condensation racing down the side.

He sighed and set his fork on the plate with the bite uneaten. Pressing his napkin to his lips, he seemed to pause and consider his words for a moment, and then his attention locked on me again. "I always had a thing for you."

I flinched. Being kind to Benji *had* sent the wrong signals. It meant more to him than to me.

"I didn't know," I said softly, giving my head a tiny shake.

He paused and glared. The angry look in his eyes told me he didn't believe me, and I sat back in my seat. "Really, I didn't know. You never told me, so how could you expect me to?"

"Come on." He brought his fist down on the table so hard the plate in front of him rattled. "It was obvious." I jolted in my seat and gaped at him in shock. "I'm sorry. It's just crazy that you didn't know. Impossible, even."

"Are you saying I'm lying?" Offended, I pushed myself into the booth back and took another drink of my water. For some reason, my mouth felt like I'd been chewing insulation, all dry and itchy.

He shook his head. "No, no, I'm just surprised is all."

I watched him settle back into his seat and pick up his forgotten bite of pancake.

"I'm just as shocked." I offered a smile that I hoped didn't wobble too much. This new development seemed like a lot to take in all at once. "Is that why you want me to work with you?"

He swallowed and pointed his fork at me. "I am worried about your safety."

But...

"But it would be nice to work with you too." He took a sip of his coffee. "Now that you're back in town and single, I thought we could see if there's still something between us."

Still? Try never. "Like I said, Benji, I just don't see us ever being more than friends."

He reached out and touched my hand. "I know you just got out of a bad relationship, but when you're ready, we can give us a go."

Was he even listening? I let out a snort. "Actually, I don't think we can, because I'm seeing someone."

His attention snapped to me as if I slapped him. "What?"

"I'm not single. While this has been fun catching up and all, I think I should go."

"Who?" He stood up as I did.

I lowered my head. "We're not public yet," I said, thinking on my feet.

Benji's hand lashed out, and his fingers locked painfully around my wrist. "Who are you seeing?" His voice rose with each word.

My face burned with the heat of embarrassment. I refused to look around and see who witnessed this humiliating moment in my life.

"That's none of your business, Benji," I said.

His eyes widened like I had no right to keep things from him, and my heart shuddered.

CHAPTER NINE

NOAH

She lied to me.

"Yo, you need to step in." Quinn nudged me under the table before looking over his shoulder at Benji and Kandra.

With a forkful of pancakes en route to my mouth, I sat frozen, struggling to process what she said loud enough for the whole diner to hear. It was just my brothers and me, an older couple, Dottie, and the cook, Oswald. Not like it was a production for the whole town, but it was still very public, and Kandra didn't like public scenes—she never had. So, this was likely driving her mad.

I could understand why Quinn thought I should step in, but I didn't.

Her words sang inside my head, ringing so loudly I couldn't hear my thoughts. *I'm seeing someone. We're not public yet.*

But she told me ...

She lied.

Pulling a deep breath through my nose, I winced as Quinn kicked me. "Are you going to do something?" He jerked his head toward where Kandra stood. Benji still clung to her wrist as if he could force her to stay against her will. She leaned away from him, staring at him in open-mouthed shock. Her expression screamed that she didn't know what to do, and my blood boiled in my veins. Every muscle in my body tensed up as if I was seconds from a fight.

Did I have the right to step in on her behalf? I wasn't her protector, or her savior, or her bodyguard. Sure, if she were in danger, I'd do something, but this was none of my damn business.

Would I cross a line if I interfered?

The bigger question was, would Benji be able to walk away if I got involved?

Her voice met my ears, but the words got lost in the slight buzz of the room. Dottie stood, shell-shocked near the kitchen, her eyes not missing a thing that happened. Behind her, Oswald offered her the phone, but she didn't take it from him. She seemed lost in her world and as unsure as I was at that moment.

"She can handle herself," Bayden said, shoving a bite of pancake into his mouth. His whole body faced forward with his shoulders hunched over his plate as if he thought someone might steal his food—a legitimate concern at this table. I'd already almost put a butter knife through Quinn's hand for trying to take one of my pancakes. The entitled brat thought he could help himself, and I wouldn't stand for it. If he'd asked nicely, it would have been a different story.

Ethan gave me a bitter glare. "Well, if you won't do something to help her, I will." He shoved his plate aside and pushed his chair back to stand up.

Anger burst in my gut, and my fork clattered onto my plate.

Ethan glanced at me as I grabbed my napkin, wiped my mouth, and prepared myself for what was about to happen.

I stood and put a hand on Ethan's chest. With a firm push, I shoved him back into his chair. He glowered at me like I was the enemy, but I could deal with him later. He wasn't stepping in to be Kandra's hero.

She wasn't mine, but she sure as hell wasn't his either.

Quinn put a hand out to stop Ethan, but my brother sat on the edge of his seat, obviously ready to leap up and step in if I screwed things up.

I approached Benji and Kandra with assured, angry steps. My work boots thudded satisfyingly on the tile floor as I moved forward. I rolled my head to loosen up my neck in case Benji got cocky and decided to try and throw a punch. I could not imagine the guy in the pink shirt hitting anything but the pile of pancakes on his plate.

Benji noticed me and let Kandra's wrist go as if she'd burned him.

She glanced over her shoulder at me, and relief flooded her expression. I promised myself I wouldn't be her hero, but I'd be her backup.

"Everything okay here?" I asked, stopping at her side and clasping my hands behind my back. Rocking up on the balls of my feet, I stared at Benji and silently dared him to give me a reason to knock his ass flat on the floor.

"I think so." Kandra rubbed her wrist as if the skin stung.

My knuckles itched. I wanted to hit Benji more than I'd wanted anything in a long time.

"Yeah, everything is fine. I was getting my breakfast to go and getting out of here." Benji let out a nervous laugh and glanced at his watch. "I've got work to do."

I gritted my teeth and glanced at Kandra while shifting back on my heels. She said it was fine, so I wasn't going to push. As much as I wanted to punch Benji, I didn't want to make her life more difficult or step over any boundaries. I hated all the complications between us. I despised this tiptoeing dishonesty that she kept up like a shield.

"If everything is fine, then," I turned as if to go back to my table. Ethan's eyes narrowed on me, and I knew he didn't agree with how I'd handled things. Quinn nodded slightly, a rolled-up pancake—one of mine, no doubt—dangling from his mouth.

Kandra's hand touched my arm. "Noah, can we talk?" Something in her voice stopped me.

"Sure." What the hell she wanted to talk about was a mystery. We had nothing more to say. Maybe it was her attempt to keep Benji at bay.

She stepped forward, and I stuck to her side. We headed for the front door, and I looked down at her. "What did you want to talk about?"

She told me with a slight shake of her head that it would have to wait until we were somewhere more private, or at least out of earshot of someone in the diner. It could be any one of them since Dottie was the town gossip, and Benji was giving her a hard time.

"Thank you," she whispered as I opened the door for her. A breeze washed over us, bringing the scent of fresh-cut grass and sun-warmed pine with it.

"For holding the door for you? You know my mother raised me right."

She smiled up at me, and my stomach tightened. "No, for stepping in back there. I know things are weird between us, but I appreciate the backup." She stopped and tucked both hands into her back pockets. With her fresh face and casual jeans and T-shirt look, she could have been seventeen again.

I glanced at the street. "You're welcome."

She shifted and pulled her hands out. "I'm sorry I screwed everything up between us." Her wistful voice warned me she was thinking things that would be bad for both of us.

"Me too."

We walked a few steps, and she lifted her face toward the sun, inhaling deeply while a smile crossed her lips.

"Why did you lie to me?" I kept my voice low and measured

because I didn't want her to think I was angry—I wasn't. I just wanted to know the truth. Why had she chosen to be dishonest?

Her eyebrows furrowed. "When did I lie to you?" Confusion contorted her features, and her lovely eyes studied me. "What are you talking about?"

"You told me you broke up with your ex." Was she going to deny it? Or try to lie again? I stopped walking and turned to face her.

She went still, then pivoted in my direction.

"I did." She spoke slowly, as if I was trying to trick her, and she was unsure of how or why I would do that. "Why would you think I lied to you about that?" Her tone took on a curious edge, without a hint of anger that I called her a liar.

I blinked. Back in the day, if I had said she lied about something, she would have bitten my head off and started world war three. She certainly wasn't the same person she'd been then.

I crossed my arms and stared her down.

The confusion in her face grew as she took in my standoffish stance, and then her eyes flicked to mine. "I didn't lie ..." She trailed off, and it was as if the switch flipped and understanding flashed in her eyes as she inhaled. "Oh, you heard me tell Benji I was seeing someone." Her shoulders slumped slightly. "I didn't lie to you."

That didn't make sense because she very clearly told Benji she was involved with someone.

She sighed as her shoulders sunk another inch. "I lied to Benji."

Why would she lie to Benji? And it hit me; she lied to ward off his advances. The bastard wasn't taking no for an answer. She had to make up something to get him to leave her the hell alone. My desire to hit him ramped up.

"I'm sorry." She touched my arms, and I lowered them. Her

finger trailed down my wrist, to my hand, and I laced my fingers with hers, giving her a reassuring squeeze, but not letting go.

"No, I'm sorry. I'm a dick." I ran a hand through my hair, pissed at myself that I accused her of lying. I was so pigheaded and couldn't see the situation for what it was, and her reaction to it.

"Well, maybe just a little." She lifted her free hand and brought her thumb and index finger close together to convey how little, and I couldn't hold back a grin.

"I want to beat him down." I was mad—mad that Kandra had to lie to Benji because he made her feel unsafe. Mad that I hadn't stepped in sooner. But mostly mad at myself that a sudden surge of protectiveness welled up in me. *You need to cool it; it isn't your job to protect her.*

"Benji?" She asked, confused again.

I nodded but needed to lighten the mood. "And my brother. The jackass stole my pancakes when I walked over to help." Despite my humor, I struggled with my need to protect her from everyone and everything that might harm her.

She laughed. "I guess I owe you pancakes, then." Her fingers tightened in mine, and I released her. Our hands slipped apart as she stared up at me with something dangerously close to affection. Her lips parted. "It's a date."

I saw something beautiful, something potentially wonderful shifting between us and had to crush it immediately. "No, it's not."

CHAPTER TEN

KANDRA

Sunday afternoon, I sat in the bedroom where I would put the nursery and stared at the walls. I pulled my thighs to my chest and planted my chin on my knees.

Questions swam in my mind. To paint or not to paint? I didn't even know the gender of the baby. What color would I choose? I hadn't done much of anything for the room except pick up a bookshelf from a discount store.

I imagined holding a baby in my arms and reading stories for hours. My eyes misted over as I pictured chasing a little toddler through the hall. I thought about making breakfast and packing lunches, and on school mornings, I'd see my little one off to the bus.

My thoughts drifted back to Noah. We saw each other every night at the bar. After our truce on the sidewalk, he talked to Roy and said it was fine to wait on his table again. It was a small step in the right direction, but a step forward, nonetheless.

We hadn't had any deep conversations since that day at the diner when he helped me escape Benji.

Tears stung my eyes as I thought about how I playfully said that my owing him pancakes was a date, and he swiftly said it wasn't.

I'd been teasing him, more joking than serious, but his biting response cut me to the bone.

Dragging the back of my hand over my eyes, I took a deep breath. Sheesh, being pregnant sure made me an emotional mess.

Before I got pregnant, I could count the number of times I cried over the last decade on one hand. But now, it seemed like everything made me cry—commercials, songs on the radio, and anything to do with babies.

I laughed at myself.

For the millionth time, I wished Noah and I had never split. Sure, I was happy to be pregnant and excited to be a mom, but all my dreams of being a parent had always included Noah. He was the one I always imagined being married to—the one I could picture spending the rest of my life with. Anthony had been nice—or so I'd thought—but he never seemed like forever material. I'd been stunned when he proposed to me, but when I thought back on that whole situation, I imagine he'd done it to hold on to me. At the time, I'd been considering leaving the modeling world behind and striking out as a photographer as I originally planned.

A strange sound in the bathroom grabbed my attention and made my body jolt. Icy-hot pinpricks danced over my skin. I stood, and a wave of light-headedness overwhelmed me. In seconds the feeling went away, and I breathed a sigh of relief that ended when the sound of trickling water met my ears.

I raced into the bathroom and found the showerhead on the tile and the spout dribbling water. I reached for the handle to turn it off, but it came off in my hand, and the rush of water increased. Without thinking about it, I put my hands over it. Half a second passed, and I realized I couldn't stop the gushing water.

With careful steps, so I wouldn't slip on the wet floor, I

dripped my way into the living room and grabbed my cell phone. I dialed the only person I knew who could help.

"Hello?" he answered.

"Bayden?" I'd called Noah's company phone, but for some reason, I'd expected Noah to answer despite knowing all four brothers ran the business together.

"Kandra?" He sounded as stunned to hear me as I was to listen to him.

"I, uh, have a problem." Rubbing the back of my neck, I paced the floor.

"Let me text you Noah's number." The line went dead, and I paced the floor. A second later, his text came through, and I sent him a silent thanks. Somehow, I felt that if Quinn had answered, I'd never hear the end of this, but Bayden kept things closer to the vest than his twin. I doubt he would tell anyone I called.

Holding my breath, I touched Noah's number on my screen. The option to call popped up and I pressed the green phone to dial. I listened to it ring and chewed on a nail while I waited. What if he didn't pick up? What if he refused to help? I pictured my whole bathroom filling with water, and a flood seeping under the door with every passing second.

"Hello?" His gruff voice made my heart flutter.

"Noah, sorry to bother you," I smiled, feeling like an idiot. Pressing my hand to my forehead, I gave my head a slight shake. "I need your help."

"Where are you?"

I bit on my lower lip and let it pop free. "My place." Oh, gosh, that sounded like a line, didn't it?

"Text me the address. I'm on my way." *Click*. I stared at my phone, stunned. He was going to help me; no questions asked. It was just a back and forth of me telling him I needed help and him saying he would be there. Imagine that.

I texted him my address and took a deep breath. My hands

trembled, and I couldn't hold back a smile. Everything had happened so fast that it only then dawned on me that calling him felt right. I could have called a plumber, or my landlord, or anyone else. Even my dad or my brother, but I didn't. I called Noah.

I walked back toward the bathroom. Thankfully, there was no river of water flowing under the door like the horrific gate scene in Titanic.

The floor was wet, but there was no ark-type flood like I had envisioned. Most of the water seemed to rush down the drain. Seeing the potential disaster somewhat contained, I relaxed a little and closed the door.

My water bill for the month would be ugly, but my house would survive.

As I padded back toward the front door to unlock it, a thought suddenly hit me—Noah would be in my house, and we would be *alone*.

We would be truly alone for the first time in over a decade.

My heart somersaulted, and I hesitated mid-step, a few feet from the door. Gritting my teeth, I reminded myself that Noah hated me before I continued walking to the door to unlock the deadbolt. When I heard his boots on the porch, I opened it and pasted a smile on my face.

"How did you get here so fast?" I asked.

"I sped. What's going on? Are you okay?" The intensity in his eyes as he studied me warmed my very soul.

"I'm fine, but let me show you what happened." I led him through the house and into the bathroom.

The second he looked at the running water, he turned and left. I chased him toward the front door. "Where are you going?"

"To my truck."

I followed him onto the porch as he walked down the path. He stopped near the street and knelt. A moment later, he walked to his truck, grabbed a few things out of the toolbox in the back of his shiny silver Super Duty, and came back my way.

I swung the door wide, and he entered with a nod. My heart skipped a beat as I followed him. The water had stopped, and I stared, puzzled.

"I turned off the water to your house at the curb. I'll turn it back on before I go." He stepped into the shower and began to work.

"Can I make you lunch or something? I appreciate you coming here without notice." I smiled at him.

"Actually, you can hold this." He tilted his head toward the shower, and I walked over. Without hesitation, he had me hold a hose while he tightened the screw thing. "You needed a new showerhead. Has it been spraying water around the head?"

I nodded, biting down on my lower lip. "I didn't know that was a sign of a problem. When I went to turn it off, the handle came loose."

He nodded. "That was a screw, and now you have a detachable showerhead. Enjoy."

"Thank you." Grateful, I squeezed my eyes closed as he leaned in close to tighten it up. We were nearly chest to chest standing there. He was so close that I could smell his warm, spicy cologne. I inhaled, loving the way I felt the body heat rolling off him.

"I'll be right back." He walked away, and I stood there, missing him suddenly and internally chewing myself out for being so stupid.

A moment later, the pipes in my house hummed to life, and I watched the showerhead, afraid Niagara Falls would set loose again, but not a drop of water leaked.

"How's it looking?" he asked from the doorway, and I jolted.

"Don't scare me like that!" I spun to face him.

"Did you test to see if it works?" He asked, ignoring me.

An evil thought crossed my mind. "Let me check." I turned the water on and pointed the nozzle at him. The spray hit him from across the room. He seemed shocked at first, but his expression darkened. I let out a squeal as he closed the distance between us and turned the showerhead on me. Warm water sprayed down my shirt while laughter rolled from my lips.

"Did you seriously spray me with water?" He was out of breath and on the brink of laughing.

"It was an accident."

"Accident my ass!" He pulled the showerhead completely from my grasp and sprayed me full force in the face. As the water quickly filled my open mouth, I spat it at him and used his surprise to wrestle the showerhead away from him. We continued to struggle as he wrapped his arms around me, and suddenly we tumbled to the wet floor in a death struggle for the slippery jet.

Giggling like crazy, I managed to spray him square in the face.

He smacked it out of my hand, and it fell back, dangling in the shower, turning in lazy circles as it sprayed.

I focused on Noah. Droplets of water clung to his dark hair and eyelashes, and those bright-blue eyes locked on my face.

My laughter went quiet as his gaze dropped to my mouth, then moved up to stare at my eyes. I inhaled between parted lips, certain he'd just thought about kissing me. My heart thundered as we stared at one another.

"I should go," he growled.

My heart sank. "You don't have to." I glanced at his mouth, dragging my tongue across my lower lip, wishing he'd lean in and kiss me.

"But I should." His eyes moved back and forth between mine like he was searching for answers. Answers I didn't have and couldn't give him. We were on my bathroom floor, soaking wet, and so close I could feel his breath cooling my chin.

I leaned in, keeping my eyes on his. He could stop me or pull away. He could if he wanted to, but he didn't move. Instead, he seemed frozen as I studied his face.

Our lips touched, and his hand came up to cup my face.

He tilted his head, and his mouth claimed mine.

CHAPTER ELEVEN

NOAH

I couldn't get yesterday's kiss out of my mind.

All I could think about were her ocean-blue eyes locked on me as she told me I didn't have to go. Her eyes moved to my mouth and said exactly what she wanted me to do instead of leave. As her tongue traced her lower lip, it left behind a sheen that woke a slumbering beast within me.

I shouldn't have kissed her, but she leaned in, pressed her lips to mine, and I was a goner. Everything flooded back. All the love, the heat, the passion. Our childhoods, sunny summers at the lake and playing in the river, camping trips under billions of stars, our first kiss...

It all swept back in one confusing, overwhelming, stunning realization. A part of me still loved her and always would, no matter how much I lied to myself.

A beep snapped me out of my thoughts as one of the trucks backed up on-site. My brothers were all off working in their respective spots, and I said a soft word of thanks they weren't here to witness my daydreaming. No doubt they'd all be able to read my mind, and I'd never hear the end of it.

We made progress on the police station; cement was poured and dry, and we were working on framing. Those were the parts I enjoyed the most, but today my head wasn't in the game because yesterday's kiss replayed repeatedly.

I was losing my damn mind. It was stupid not to keep my distance, but the panic in Kandra's voice when she'd called alarmed me. How could I tell her no? I was worried she was hurt, and my instinct to protect her kicked in before I thought about the potential consequences.

The guys worked to raise a frame, and I hurried over to lend more stability as the bones of the walls were lifted. With shouts of joy, the men got to work securing it while others nodded or watched. I locked eyes with each of my brothers in turn. Quinn flashed me a quick grin, while Bayden gave a stoic nod. Ethan glanced up into the sky, where the clouds parted just enough to allow the sun to break through. I expected him to tell me Dad approved of everything we were doing.

As we secured the frames into place, I backed off, needing some time before my brothers descended on me like the wolves the bastards were. I didn't get ten feet away before a hand clamped down on my shoulder. I turned to face Quinn.

"Well?" He arched an eyebrow, and my stomach twisted.

"Well, what?" I could play dumb, but we both knew I wasn't fooling him for a second.

He glanced at Bayden, who strolled up to us. "How did last night's house call go?" His calm tone had my knuckles itching to rearrange his face. Of course, he told them she called for me.

His steel-toed boot shifted the gravel as I spoke.

"I don't know, how's the sheriff?"

He lifted his shoulders, giving me a wicked half grin. "Don't know; haven't seen her, but we're talking about you. Try to keep up." He patted my chest as Ethan approached on my left.

"Has he explained, yet?" Ethan seemed worried he'd missed out on some news.

"What is with you guys? You're like a bunch of high school girls gossiping in the bathroom." Annoyed, I turned to go, but they broke and re-formed a circle around me. With my exit cut off, I hesitated.

"So, it went well, then?" Quinn's eyes sparkled. "If nothing happened, you'd just say that."

"Nothing happened," I growled the lie right to my brothers' faces, but I could see the suspicious looks in their eyes. They didn't believe me, and rightly so.

"Oh, it was something big." Quinn tapped Bayden's arm while staring at me, and Bayden sidestepped his reach.

"Don't you guys have work to do?" This familiar dance was becoming commonplace, and I didn't like it one bit. It was none of their damn business what happened between Kandra and me. Still, thinking about it, even though I wasn't talking about it, brought up questions. Why had she called me? Was she looking for a way to drag me back into her life? Was it all a ruse to kiss me and make me remember the past? If so, she succeeded. It couldn't possibly be that I was the first person to come to mind in a moment of panic. Or, if I was, it was because I was likely the most polarizing person in her life at the moment.

"Probably, but you're our brother, and we need to check in on your well-being. Especially when your ex calls looking for you in a panic. What happened, anyway?" Bayden seemed more curious than his usual disinterested self.

"Plumbing mishap."

Quinn's eyes widened. "What did you do about it?"

"Took care of it and went home."

Ethan's lips tugged into a slight grin. "Plumbing, huh? Is that what you old-timers are calling it nowadays?"

"You're only two years younger than I am. And no, it was an actual plumbing problem, you pervert. Can I go now?" Without waiting for an answer, I walked toward my truck and grabbed my coffee thermos. After pouring a cup of the steaming black liquid, I took a sip, which scalded all sensation from my tongue as Quinn spoke again.

"Well, it's a good sign that she calls you in case of an emergency. Maybe there's still something there, eh?" He elbowed me in the ribs and coffee sloshed over the cup's rim to burn my fingers.

"I will throw this at you," I warned, and he danced a step to the side like a nervous horse.

"I hope you're nicer to her than you are to me, or you'll never win her back." He turned to leave, and I yelled to his retreating back.

"I don't want her back." Even as I said the words, a sense of unease swept through me. Was that true?

"I don't think you mean that."

I nearly jumped out of my skin, and white-hot pinpricks raced up and down my body as I spun to face Ethan. More of my coffee spilled, but this time I managed to evade the volcanic liquid.

Ethan wasn't staring at me; he had his iPad in hand and was gazing at it, likely making adjustments to some other project he had stored away.

"Mean what?" My tongue ached, and I wondered if it would blister from the coffee burn. That would be just my damn luck lately.

His hand stilled, and his eyes flicked over the top of the tablet to mine. "That you don't want Kandra back."

I let out a sharp chuckle. "You guys aren't letting this go, are you?"

"Nah. We care about you, so we want to be here for you, but you make that hard as hell, brother." His attention returned to his tablet. "Besides, I think you're already in over your head with her. I'm not sure you ever climbed out of the deep end with that one."

I dumped out the rest of my coffee and screwed the cap back on. I'd lost all taste for it, not that I'd be able to taste it anyway after scalding every taste bud to death.

"I'm not in love with her if that's what you think." I tossed the thermos on the passenger seat of my truck.

He snorted. "Okay. Keep lying to yourself, but we all know better." He lowered the iPad and gave me his undivided attention.

I closed my truck door and stood for a moment while considering all exit strategies. "What are you working on?" Maybe I could derail him by getting him to talk about work.

"Top secret project. Try again." He grinned.

"Try what again?" I gave as innocent of an expression as I could while leaning back against my truck.

He frowned. "Try changing the subject again. You're terrible at not giving yourself away. Maybe you should work on that." With that, he walked away.

I wasn't fooling any of them. Damn.

The memory of Kandra's big blue eyes as she leaned in to kiss me rose in my mind once more. I let out a soft curse and walked away from my truck. I would get hurt again. I wasn't enough for her all those years ago, so why would that have changed now? If it did, was her settling for me something I could live with?

I glanced at the sky. "I could use some advice, Dad." A profound sense of loss filled me, and I found myself missing him more than ever. Not just because I wanted his counsel, but because I missed the man who was my hero.

Of course, there was no answer save the sound of men working behind me—not that I expected anything else. No, I had a feeling I'd been right at the start. It was best to avoid Kandra.

"You coming back to work?" Quinn waved me over, and I

walked toward him. There were things to do, and I didn't have time to wallow in self-pity and wonder about *what-ifs* or *if-onlys*.

Maybe if I put my back into a few hours of hard work, I could forget my problems, forget Kandra's kiss, and forget how much I missed my dad.

I stood next to Quinn, aware he was staring at me intently.

"If you need to jet out of here, I'll cover for you," Quinn said.

I gawked at him. "Why, did something happen?" My heart thundered as worry swept over me. Was it Mom? What had I missed?

He gave his head a slow side to side shake. "Nothing happened, but that's the same look you had on your face at Dad's funeral. If you need time, go. We've got this."

"Nah, I need the distraction. Might head out a bit early to pick up groceries though." My fridge was looking pretty pathetic. This morning my breakfast options were a beer, an old opened bottle of water, and various condiments. I didn't like to shop, but I wanted to eat, so sacrifices needed to be made.

"That's fine." Despite his assurance, I noticed him eyeing me as we threw ourselves into work. It wasn't just him keeping tabs on me. Bayden and Ethan watched me much more closely than usual. Tuning them out, I focused on the job. Everywhere an extra set of hands was needed, I volunteered.

"Slow down, brother, or you'll make us look bad," Bayden said, handing me a nail gun.

I chuckled. "Get to work then, you lazy bastard."

"He resembles that remark," Ethan said.

And for a little while, it was like old times before Kandra came back and before Dad died. Back when everything was easy.

When it was finally time for me to duck out, I got in my truck and closed the door, and breathed a sigh of relief. My body was sore from the hard work, but it was the exhaustion in my mind that stuck out.

A couple of the guys waved, and even though my arm seemed to weigh a thousand pounds, I returned the gesture.

As I geared up to shop, I promised myself I'd keep it short and get home to relax from all the stress of the day.

CHAPTER TWELVE

KANDRA

I glanced into the cart, trying to figure out what other adult purchases I could add to keep it from looking like I was a twelve-year-old with dangerous amounts of money and a serious junk food habit.

Among chocolate-covered granola bars, chocolate peanut butter cups, red velvet ice cream, grasshopper cookies, and pickles, I'd throw in some lettuce, salad fixings, fresh broccoli for iron, and a bag of easy-peel oranges.

My cart still looked like it was filled by a child pretending to be an adult, and it was becoming questionable. With a sigh, I added apples and wondered if I should get rid of some of the sugary treats so I didn't give away the fact that I was eating for two. It was important no one knew about my pregnancy because I needed time to come to terms with it myself before I had to field questions from the inquiring minds of Cross Creek.

Thoughts of a certain tall, dark-haired, handsome man filled my head. I tried to shove them away, but the sensation of his lips on mine was so intense, I lifted my fingers to my mouth as if I could still feel him.

"You look deep in thought." As if he'd stepped from my thoughts into the aisle, Noah studied me with a slight curve at the corners of his lips.

I gawked at him in shock. What were the odds? I'd been thinking about him kissing me, and he appeared—poof—like a genie had granted me a wish. The chances were pretty good, actually, with how much I'd been thinking about him lately and the fact that we lived in a small town, bumping into one another was almost inevitable. Besides, I didn't believe in genies.

"Yeah, trying to remember what else I need." I smiled, hoping I covered up my surprise well enough.

He let out a deep chuckle, and the rich sound sent a tremble down my spine. "You never were one for lists."

"Still don't use them. Maybe I should start, but then I'd have to remember to bring it with me and ..." No way would I tell him that lately, my shopping was driven by cravings and not necessity.

He leaned in close as if to impart some wisdom, and out of the corner of his mouth, he said, "I don't use a list either."

I opened my mouth in mock disbelief. "No."

At my serious tone, he chuckled, and I let out a giggle. It should have been strange, awkward, or uncomfortable, but this was easy. We had kissed, so why weren't things more complicated?

He steered his cart next to mine and picked up mushrooms. With that and the eggs in his cart, I could hazard a guess. "Omelets?"

He nodded.

That sounded delicious. "I might have to come to your place for breakfast."

He went still and studied me.

A moment later, I realized what he thought I was saying.

"I should go." Mortified at my slip-up, I grabbed my cart and headed for the next aisle. Why did I keep saying stupid things to him?

I moved forward, trying to get my rapid heartbeat under control. A cart moved next to mine, and I glanced into Noah's eyes. "I knew what you meant."

My cheeks heated, even with his reassurance. "It just sounded bad. I keep tripping over my tongue around you."

"I think it's kind of cute." As he said the words, something flashed behind his eyes. Something almost like anger. Was he mad at his words or his feelings?

"Thank you. That makes me feel better." I wanted to diffuse the situation as quickly as possible. It was nice hearing he thought my slips were cute, and it made me less self-conscious.

He nodded and moved on.

I watched him retreat with heaviness in my heart. I'd missed him a lot more than I ever realized. Being here, seeing him, listening to him talk, and noticing that light in his eyes when he looked at me, it all came rushing back.

As glad as I was at how my life had gone, and how much I treasured the experiences I lived, I wished I hadn't hurt him all those years ago with my careless and untrue words. I wanted him back, but I wasn't sure that was possible.

I moved through the store, grabbing things at random, and thinking about making lists. I needed to get my life together. I could make a plan of action and live it out, including a strategy to win Noah back. Or at least try to let him know that I still loved him and wanted to be with him. I messed up and knew it.

With fresh confidence, I walked to the register and unloaded my groceries. The cashier smiled, "I get cravings too," she lowered her voice and glanced around as my heart raced, "when it's that time." She whispered the last part, and I let out the breath I held.

I lifted the box of cookies. "I'm glad somebody gets it." I smiled a conspiratorial smile. *If she only knew.*

After I paid, I stepped into the sunshine and headed for my

car, only to find Noah loading up his truck, which was nose to nose with my car.

"Howdy, stranger," I said with a twang.

He glanced up and walked his empty cart to the stall before returning to help load my car. "Long time, no see."

Past him was Max, whose smile took up half his face.

Noah glanced over and waved and then returned to loading my car.

"Why is there a boxed bookshelf in the back seat?" he looked at me, and I weakly lifted my shoulders.

The bookshelf was for the baby's room, but the dang thing weighed too much for me to lift; a fact I hadn't known because someone else loaded it into the car for me when I bought it. I didn't notice how heavy it was until I got home.

With a bag dangling from his hand, he studied me intently.

Staring at the floor so he couldn't catch the lie in my eyes, I answered.

"Haven't gotten around to unloading it yet." That seemed like as good of an excuse as any. His serious expression said I wasn't fooling him for a second.

I might suck at lists, but nothing could hold me back when I had a project in mind. It had been driving me nuts that I hadn't started or finished.

Of course, I could open the box and take it in a piece at a time, but with how tired I'd been, and how many hours I worked, it didn't seem likely.

"And it's heavy. If I get hurt, I might miss work and get fired." That seemed plausible and bordered on the truth.

He placed the bag on the car's floorboard behind the driver's seat and picked up another and walked it around the car to set it on the other side. Thankful he wasn't asking more questions but aware he was watching me closely, I refused to look him in the eyes.

Would he spot the truth if I stared directly at him? Would he see right through me as Max had done? Noah always had a knack for knowing what I was thinking, and I'd thought it was sweet when we were younger. Now, as a woman with secrets, it scared the crap out of me.

"I really like my job. And Roy. Like I said, I want to make the best out of my life, and having a job is important." Maybe if I could defend my reason, he'd believe it.

"You don't have to explain yourself to me." He put the last bag in my car and closed the door. As he put away my cart, I stood by my driver's side door and watched him.

He'd grown into a powerful man, the stuff of dreams, someone who could rival any Hollywood hunk.

He walked back with an effortless swagger. "Why didn't you say something the other day? I would have helped you set up the bookshelf."

Was that what he'd been puzzling over? Maybe he hadn't figured me out after all.

"Oh, I couldn't ask you to do that. Besides, I'd already bothered you enough that day, and then we..." Cutting off the word before I could say kissed, I cleared my throat and glanced around, remembering the small-town gossip thing. "I didn't want to be an inconvenience or make things more awkward than I already had." I looked at him and offered a slight smile.

The bright blue sky behind him highlighted his eyes and gave his hair an inky blue tint. A devilish grin showed his pearly whites, and he lifted both shoulders. "It's not weird for me. Is it for you?"

Weird didn't even begin to define what this was for me. Strange and wonderful and scary all at the same time.

"I don't want to be a bother." I already called him to help fix the showerhead. Besides, would he guess I was setting up a nursery? There wasn't much of anything in there, but could he figure it out based on what I had?

I just wasn't ready to tell him. Maybe I wasn't ready to face my truth. I was a dumped, has-been model, a soon to be single mom who worked slogging drinks at a bar. I left to become more and ended up back where I started. Only now, I had regrets.

Why couldn't I tell him? Ignoring that whispering internal question, I saw the light in his eyes, refusing to take no for an answer.

"It can't sit in the back of your car forever, and I don't want to see you get hurt. I'll run home, drop my stuff off, and swing by your place to set it up."

I opened my mouth to protest, but he held up a hand. "I have the rest of the day off, anyway, and nothing to do. Helping you will keep me busy."

How could I argue with that?

"Thank you," I said.

"You're welcome." With that, he turned and headed to his truck, then looked at me past the door. "Be there in about fifteen."

I had fifteen minutes to get home and make sure there was nothing incriminating around. As his truck fired to life, I got behind the wheel but waited for him to drive off before backing carefully out of my spot. I didn't want him to know I was in a hurry.

As I drove, I thought about his words. He said he couldn't have me getting hurt, and that warmed my heart. His protective expression sent butterflies through my belly.

Yep, I was still in love with Noah.

CHAPTER THIRTEEN

NOAH

I parked next to her little car, turned off the engine, and steeled myself. For the second time in a few days, I would be alone with her in her home.

Last time she kissed me. This time I'd be more careful to keep my distance. Not because I didn't want to kiss her—I did—but because I needed to stop being blind where she was concerned. She'd broken my heart once, and I wasn't letting that happen again.

Her door opened, and she stepped out, with that fresh smile on her face. The light breeze caught her floral blouse, and it fluttered around her frame as her black pants clung to her legs. In her bare feet and makeup-free face, it was like ten years never passed, and I couldn't stop staring.

She hurried over and opened her car as I tore my gaze away from her and focused on the task at hand. I lifted the box, flipped it up on my shoulder, and carried it toward the front door. Her soft intake of breath didn't escape me, nor did the sensation of her eyes heating my flesh.

"Are you objectifying me?" I teased and looked over my shoulder.

She giggled, her cheeks turning a darker shade of pink. "Has anyone told you that you should be in one of those *buff dudes snuggling kittens* calendars?"

Nope. Nobody had ever told me that. I didn't work out to look good; I worked out because my job demanded physical strength.

Without another word, she raced ahead and led me through her home to the second bedroom. I set the bookshelf down in the middle of the room and turned to her. "This is the room you want it in?"

Her teeth worried her lower lip as she nodded. My attention locked on her lips, and the thought of how soft they were when they touched mine. Her kiss had been sweet and innocent—almost afraid.

I hadn't held back. That day I pressed my tongue to the seam of Kandra's lips and demanded entry, and she obliged. When her tongue swept across her lower lip, I snapped out of my thoughts. I wasn't kissing her again.

"Did you want anything to drink? A snack?" Her soft voice seemed to offer more than food, but I ignored the tug in me and smiled at her.

"Water would be fine." Anything to get her out of the room and give me a moment to gather my composure.

The second she left, I pulled out my pocketknife and cut open the box. Upending the contents onto the floor, I sorted the pieces.

She returned with the water and a cheerful, "Here you go."

Thanking her and taking a grateful gulp, I lost myself in the build because, otherwise, I might lose myself in her, and that wouldn't be wise. Not now. Not ever.

She watched me put things into neat piles and picked up the instructions. The sweet scent of her—fresh citrus and something flowery—filled my nose. After a look at the parts, I knew I'd need Allen wrenches.

I stood up, and she stared up at me with a worried look in her eyes.

"Need to grab my tools," I said.

A wicked light twinkled in her eyes, and a smile crept across her face. "I have tools, too."

"I'm familiar with my tools, so I'll just go grab them." As I left the room, I heard her huff that I used to be familiar with her tools. I couldn't hold back a grin even as my brain warned me this would not end well. I needed to be cooling things off, not letting innuendos and thoughts of kissing fire me up.

Leaving the house, I hurried to my truck and grabbed my toolbox before heading back. Max was filling a mailbox across the street and gave me a wave. I nodded and lifted the toolbox as if that was a good enough excuse to be at her place.

He winked, which told me he wasn't fooled for a second.

Inside, I found her right where I left her, but now she was sprawled out on the floor, reading the instructions with a puzzled expression on her face. "Please tell me you understand these." She handed me the page, and I glanced over the words and diagrams.

"Nope, not in English, but I build houses for a living. I mean, how hard can this be?"

She breathed a visible sigh of relief. "I'm pretty sure we don't even have the right hardware." Her fingers gripped the little bag, and I peeked into it. She was right, not even close.

"I have all kinds of spare parts, and we can work with what they gave us. We'll figure this out." I wasn't the least bit worried. With quick hands, I moved wooden joints together and took her hands in mine. Showing her where to hold things, and ignoring the tingle of her touch, I worked screws into place. Within ten minutes, the basic frame was in place, and she let out a soft sound of surprise.

"That was fast." She touched my hand as I held the shelf in place and bent over to fit the bracket where it belonged. The touch arced like electricity in me, and I tried to pretend I didn't feel it as she inhaled.

I needed to get this done and get out of here before something happened that I couldn't take back.

"Thank you for doing this." She smiled at me, drawing my attention back to her full lips. There was something so inviting about her, so beautiful and enticing, and I wanted to lean in and kiss her, but kissing her wasn't wise. "You're welcome."

With the last bolt in place, I picked up a rag she'd left sitting over a chair, wiped down the unit, and then set it upright. I scanned the room before glancing at her. "Where do you want it?"

She looked around the room. "I'm not quite sure."

Something didn't ring true as I watched her think. Just like at the store when she'd given me a couple of crap reasons why she hadn't already set up the bookshelf.

The Kandra I knew could out lift some of the guys and would never shy away from hard work. She also never started a project she didn't fully intend to finish quickly.

"What is the plan for this room?" I asked, thinking that might help her figure out where to put it. Standing up, I stretched my back a bit.

"Um," she bit down on her lip. "I just need someplace to put my books."

Again, something didn't feel right about her answer. She was always a planner—except when grocery shopping—and that wasn't a quality people just changed.

"How about over there?" I gestured to the right of the window, in case she decided she wanted to sit under the window to read. "You could put a comfortable chair under the window for the natural light and read."

Her expression lit up. "I love that!" She bounced to her feet and wrapped her arms around my shoulders.

With her soft body pressed to the front of me and her lips too close for comfort, I struggled for control. Giving her an awkward pat on the shoulder, I tried to ignore how good her curves felt against me. I turned my head to study the spot. Meanwhile, I talked my body down from a potentially embarrassing reaction as her fragrance filled my lungs.

She let me go after what seemed like decades, and with an internal sigh of relief, I picked up the wooden shelving and moved it effortlessly to the spot.

"It's perfect." Her exuberant tone lifted my spirits even as I wondered if I'd ever really known her at all, but that wasn't the truly troubling part. Despite knowing better, I wanted to get to know her again, and I was sure that made me a fool.

With the bookshelf in place, I turned to face her and found eyes lit with warmth and desire that hit me like a sledgehammer to the gut.

"Thank you again," she whispered. "I couldn't have done it without you."

Despite that *something's not quite right* feeling still churning in my gut, I nodded. "You're welcome." The unintentionally husky quality of my voice must have had a visceral effect, causing goosebumps to race up and down her arms. The hollow at the base of her throat bottomed out, and a visible shiver ran down her spine.

My eyes dropped to her perfect mouth again, then met hers once more.

Her lips parted, and her gaze searched my face as if I had the answers she needed, but I wasn't even sure what the questions were. Something delicate in her expression took me back to the old days: Our first kiss, the first time I'd held her close, the sensation of her peach-soft skin on mine. I recalled how hard we loved, how easily we'd fallen, and how perfect she always felt in my arms. She looked at me like I was the piece missing from her life; she made me believe everything would be fine as long as I had her, and there were a million other little things that made me fall for her, and without thinking, I closed the distance between us.

She stood there with excitement flickering in her incredible eyes and watched me approach. I pulled her into my arms, and she looked at me as if asking what would happen next. I didn't have words to offer because this wasn't planned.

"Noah," she whispered.

My name on her lips sent arousal bolting through every inch of my being, and I let out a little growl. Lost in memories, I lowered my lips to hers and swallowed her soft breath of surprise. My tongue slid along her lower lip. She whimpered and opened to me without hesitation.

My whole body responded to her, and my core tightened with lust. I strained against the front of my pants, every fiber of my being tensing.

She let out a soft moan of pleasure as my tongue swirled around hers, then ravaged her mouth.

Her arms slipped up around my shoulders, and she clung to me as if she'd fall if I weren't holding her. I'd wanted to kiss her all day, but I battled those feelings.

This was a terrible idea, but we were adults. The heart wanted what it wanted, and right now, that was Kandra.

So what if she had hurt me? We could start over, start fresh, try again. This time, there'd be no secrets between us. I'd find out exactly what she needed, and we'd figure out how to build something together because I wanted Kandra in my life.

It was stupid to think I could fight this, and I was done trying.

She was mine.

CHAPTER FOURTEEN

KANDRA

With his lips on mine, he scooped me up. After a small squeak of surprise, I wrapped my legs around his hips as he carried me toward my bedroom. He pushed the door open with his elbow, and seconds later, lowered me onto my bed. Clinging to him, I gasped as he broke the kiss.

His weight pressed between my thighs while delicious sensations spread like liquid warmth through my core. Staring up into his earnest eyes, I sensed his hesitation. Was he waiting for me to tell him something?

A nagging thought that I needed to tell him the truth filled me, but I couldn't form the words.

"Do you want this?" he asked gently.

His need for my consent made my heart swell, and I nodded. "I do."

The second the words left my lips, he leaned in and kissed me again. My hands flattened to his abs, and the sensation of steel under smooth skin sent my heart into overdrive. His tongue tickled my lips, and I opened for him as I slid my hands up his chest, pulling his shirt up with them.

He broke the kiss and yanked it off. With him leaning over me, powerful and restrained with white-hot passion in his eyes, I couldn't breathe. He captured the hem of my shirt, and I wiggled and raised a few inches as he slipped it over my head and flung it on the floor.

He stared at me for a heartbeat, then another. Worry began to creep in. Could he tell?

"You're beautiful." With that growl, he lowered and kissed my throat, my collarbone, my shoulder. I clung to him, loving the heat of his skin on mine.

"I've missed you so damn much." His lips came back to mine, but only for a second before tagging my chin, my jaw, and finally tickling my earlobe.

"You've always been the one for me." The tip of his tongue traced the hollow at the base of my throat, and my heart thundered so hard I could hear the pulse in my ears. It was so loud I worried I wouldn't hear the next thing he said. I wanted to absorb every word, sop up every bit of love, and inhale every sweet thing because I'd been desperately missing love like this. Noah never loved me in halves, or bits, or pieces. He'd loved me whole; the good, the bad, the shameful. He loved me when I failed, and when I was at my best, he just loved *me*.

He kissed down my belly and slipped off my pants. His fingertips brushed lightly up my thighs, along my hips, and he pressed his mouth to my stomach. Over the spot between my hips, he gave a gentle little love nip that brought an army of goosebumps to life. I loved that he was in charge, that he was so focused on me, that I felt like the center of his world.

He kissed his way up my stomach again, making a little circle around my belly button that brought a smile to my lips. I studied his serious face and ran my fingers through his hair.

This was what I'd missed, his absolute worship. Nobody had

ever loved me as Noah had. Nobody had ever been so engrossed in me.

He lifted his head and flashed a sexy, heated smile. "What's that grin for, love?"

My heart melted, and I struggled against my emotions. "You."

He let out a low sound deep in his throat and lowered his head again. His tongue tasted the vee between my ribs and then kissed the line between my breasts until he was back at my lips.

I opened for him without hesitation. The heated length of him brushed my inner thigh, and I quivered in excitement.

Our bodies fit together like we were made for each other. Despite our need for one another, Noah was gentle, kind, and loving with every motion, every movement, every touch.

He broke the kiss, and I groaned.

"Are you okay?" he whispered into my ear.

I nodded, unable to trust my voice. But it was a lie; I was better than okay. I'd never been so good in my life.

"I've missed you so much." I wound my arms around his shoulders, and his brilliant gaze locked on my face. "I am so sorry I hurt you all those years ago. I know they say the grass is greener on the other side, but that couldn't be further from the truth, and I had no idea what I would be missing when I left. From that moment I said no, I knew I had made a mistake, but I also knew I couldn't just come crawling back like nothing had happened because the pain I had caused was too much. I tried to forget you—forget us—but you never forget where your heart is. I did the best I could to move on, but once I came back, I realized that I had spent the last ten years living someone else's life, while my life was here, with you." I regretted it with every fiber of my being. "I know I can never fix it—"

With a soft sound, he kissed me again, cutting off my words. When he finally released my lips, he pressed his forehead to mine. His breaths washed over me as we moved together in unison. "I forgive you. We were young when you left, and I now understand why you did. It took me the entire time you were gone, but I realize now, you just needed to find yourself. You said you aren't the same person now as you were then, and I see that. I know the time away was just as hard on you as it was me. But I think we both grew during that time, and the fact that you came back to me lets me know we are right where we are supposed to be."

My heart raced. "Are you saying—?"

"I don't hate you. I never hated you."

Heat engulfed my chest as he moved gently, flooding my body with incredible sensations and loving warmth. I breathed a sigh of relief at his words. Everything was right in the world. Being with him, even after so much time had passed, felt right. Being in his arms was like coming home, and there was nowhere I'd rather be.

"I never stopped loving you," I whispered the words, and he planted a quick kiss on my lips.

"I never stopped loving you either."

I couldn't hold back my joy; it spilled forth and found a home on my lips. I must have looked stupid, smiling like a fool, because he chuckled and gave me another quick kiss.

"You're incredible, and I'm glad you're finally home." His whisper warmed me, and I held him tighter. I finally found where I belonged—in his arms, and I never wanted to leave again.

Every touch pushed me closer to the edge as I clung to him, desperate for purchase. He lowered, bringing his heated skin to mine. My eyes closed, indulging in the sensation of his weight on me, his skin on mine, and the sheer love pouring between us as he moved.

"I don't want this to be a onetime thing." His words sent a delicious thread of delight through me. "I need you in my life and want you by my side."

I wanted all the same things. "Yes, please," I whispered, still worried my voice would give out. The threat of tears—happy-everything-is-perfection tears, not sad tears—loomed close, and I blinked to keep them back. I refused to cry.

His lips met mine, and I kissed him back, desperate for the closeness. Our tongues danced as our bodies moved. As the sensations and excitement built in me, my core wound tighter and tighter, building toward the promise of release.

"You're mine," he growled, and I whimpered in agreement. I wanted to be his. I wanted his brand of loving, his kindness, his protective nature. I wanted everything about Noah Lockhart. With every motion, every word, every gentle kiss he planted on my lips, I wanted more, needed more. I needed him—all of him.

And as his body moved, my hips rocked harder, demanding more while soft whimpering sounds of pleasure escaped my mouth. His teeth gently scraped my neck, and then his velvety lips tickled my earlobe again. The sensations crashed over me, taking my ability to think with them.

He lifted to look me in the eyes once more, then planted a quick kiss on my lips. "You're so perfect," he murmured, not even bothering to remove his lips from mine. Him talking so close tickled my mouth, and my heart slammed hard against my ribs. So hard, I wondered if he could feel the thumping.

My vision blurred, and dots of color danced behind my eyes as pleasure washed over me.

Noah held me close, his words sinking into my cells. "I've got you. You're okay."

I knew I'd be okay as long as he held me. He would keep me safe, and I'd always be loved. Everything would work out.

With his warm skin on mine, locked in the safety of his embrace, I let myself go in a way I'd never been able to do with anyone else. Lost in emotions, I enjoyed the rapid climb to the top, and then the slow, intense drop that ended with him shuddering in my arms. Clutching him, I reveled in how he warmed me up from the inside out.

For a second, I could pretend everything was perfect. I could imagine I wasn't lying to him. I could act like I hadn't let this happen without telling him the truth.

He moved beside me and held me close. With his powerful arms around me, I tried not to get stuck in my head, though my thoughts spun around. Did that really just happen? I knew I'd messed up badly, and I wasn't sure if I could come back from this mistake.

"Did you mean it?" I whispered, needing to know where I stood and hoping for some internal guidance on what to do next. Maybe he didn't mean it. It could have been pillow talk.

But did that make what I'd done any less terrible? Almost hating myself, I pressed a palm to my forehead as he lifted on one elbow and smiled down at me.

"Every word. Didn't you?" The hopeful excitement in his eyes made me ache all over.

I nodded, my throat closing up so tightly tears sprung to my eyes. I had also meant every word, but things were complicated.

Why wasn't I honest from the start and tell him the news that first day? I held it back like it wasn't anyone's business but my own.

"I did everything I could to stay away from you." His fingertips trailed up and down my side while his eyes followed their movement. The tickling sensation gave me tingles, but I loved the feeling. "I couldn't do it." Affectionate eyes met mine. "It's always been you, Kandra. I knew it, and my brothers knew it. I was just too stubborn and pigheaded to admit it to myself or anyone else."

A smile tugged the corners of my lips. "You? Stubborn? No." Even my light teasing fell a little bit flat, but he still chuckled.

"I know. I've been trying to work on it." He seemed to study my face for a moment, and I knew he could see I still had some secrets. We always had a way of reading each other. Looking away, I tried to keep my heart from breaking. It was all so perfect, so beautiful, but so utterly hopeless. I'd screwed us up before we even had a chance all because I hadn't been honest from the start.

"I'm not in a hurry. There's no rush. I'll be here when you're ready, even if you need some time." His loving words told me he had no idea what was going on, but his message and kindness put a crack in my heart because he was wrong. He wouldn't be here when I was ready, because I betrayed him.

I'd slept with him without telling him I was pregnant with another man's baby.

How could I fix that? How could he ever trust me after he found out? I didn't deserve a man as wonderful and loving as Noah.

CHAPTER FIFTEEN

NOAH

She was still asleep when I slipped out of bed and quickly dressed. With light steps and a happy heart, I made my way into the kitchen. I would swear months had passed with everything that had happened last night, but it was just Thursday.

Opening up the fridge, I pulled out eggs and milk to make her either the fluffiest scrambled eggs with cheese or an omelet for breakfast. I found a container of feta and some baby spinach and took those out along with the butter.

I moved around her kitchen, feeling more at home than I'd felt in a long time. Warming up the cast iron skillet, I had to smile. Throwing butter in the pan, I let it heat while I cracked the eggs into a bowl and found a whisk to beat them.

All the while, I couldn't get thoughts of her or last night out of my head. She wanted us to be together, and I wasn't going to get in my own way and screw up a good thing. Max was right; someone would snatch her up, and I wanted that someone to be me, so I would treat her right and love her in ways she has never been loved before.

With the eggs whisked and the butter sizzling, I emptied the bowl into the pan and dusted it with salt and pepper. My mother taught us that cooking was love, and she made sure every one of her boys could feed themselves. She didn't believe cooking was a woman's job and called that silly viewpoint *nonsense,* and I agreed with her.

At the sink, I noticed a scrub brush with bristles circling it and a rounded sponge on top. I needed to ask Kandra where she got it because one of those would work perfectly for all those glasses I couldn't fit my hand in to wash or my thermos. Putting the bowl in the sink, I rinsed the spinach, carried the wet leaves back to the counter, and continued to make her breakfast. Sprinkling feta on the perfect egg and spinach mixture, I watched it melt and marveled at how much I enjoyed making her breakfast. This was something I could get used to—wanted to get used to.

As I cleaned up, I thought about how beautiful she looked, how peaceful her features had been when I slipped out of bed. I couldn't get the big dumb grin off my face. Everything was finally going my way, and I couldn't be happier. The scent of the cheese hit my nose, and I thought maybe I'd missed something like garlic or diced onion to make it perfect, but I hadn't seen any in the house.

With a shrug, I made a mental note to pick some up for her. Carrying the dishes I had dirtied to the sink, I hand washed them and stacked them on the drying rack.

There was no way I would leave the place a mess. On the counter, next to the sink, was a little rack with lots of arms. My brow furrowed as I puzzled over it. The best I could come up with was a sponge dryer or a shot glass holder?

If it was the latter, I'd have to have a talk with her about her drinking problem. I chuckled. I didn't give a damn if she had a shot glass rack, but the thing looked pitifully empty. Maybe I needed to pick her up a set of glasses for it. With the last dish washed, I wiped the edge of the counter and headed back to the omelet.

While I put it in the microwave to keep it warm, I wondered how I would break the news to my brothers? What would my mother say? While I knew my brothers would tease me, I also had a feeling they'd be happy for us. After all, they'd been pushing so hard this couldn't possibly come as a surprise.

It might be a tougher sell to my mother. Kandra hurt me when we split, and Mom might go all lioness on her.

I scanned the cleaned kitchen. Everything had come together quickly, but I wasn't ready to wake her yet, so I filled the coffeepot with water and looked around for the grounds.

Within minutes, the fragrant smell of coffee filled the air. I pulled a couple of mugs from the cabinet and set them down before going on a hunt for cream and sugar.

In the fridge, I found sugar cookie flavored creamer. Who wanted sugar cookie flavored coffee? With a shrug, I added it to both mugs and stood back, inhaling the smell of a good morning. There was nothing quite like a good hot cup of coffee first thing in the AM.

I glanced toward the bedroom, wondering if I should wake her or let her sleep a bit longer. I wanted to wake her up because I wanted to spend more time with her. Part of me was worried about how she'd feel if she woke up and realized I wasn't there. Would she think I'd crept out in the middle of the night like a coward?

All the worry and self-doubt bothered me. I wasn't the type to get so worked up. I'd never been hung up on a woman before her and hadn't been hung up on any woman after. Settling down hadn't been in the cards.

Lifting the ceramic mug to my lips, I breathed it in and let the essence float over my senses. The sweet and bitter balance seemed nice. I glanced toward her bedroom door again, then took a scalding sip. I was always burning myself lately. I raced for the freezer to grab an ice cube for my coffee.

On the fridge were pictures of her and her mother hugging.

Kandra looked so much like her mom, and I knew she was excited to be close to her again. The two of them were inseparable before she left.

A soft sound from the bedroom alerted me that Kandra must be up. The bathroom door closed, and my heart beat faster. Would things be awkward between us because of last night? Would she regret any of it, or could we pick up where we left off?

Nervous and excited, I took another sip of coffee and waited.

The water in the bathroom ran, and I remembered the day I fixed the showerhead. I couldn't keep a smile off my face.

She walked into the kitchen, saw me, and froze. For a second, she just stood there before a smile crossed her lips. "Good morning," she said, opening her arms to me.

I stepped in and hugged her, inhaling the sweet scent of her hair. "Good morning. You didn't think I took off, did you?"

She lifted her shoulders. "It crossed my mind."

"Not a chance. I made you breakfast." I let her go and turned toward the microwave. After heating it for thirty seconds, I offered it to her.

A stunned look crossed her face. "Thank you." There was an odd, breathy quality to her voice that caught my attention.

"There's also coffee, but it's burning in hell hot." I carried the mug I'd filled for her to the table and set it down.

She smiled sweetly, then glanced at the food. Something in her expression shifted, and the sudden urge to smooth over an awkward moment filled me. "I know you love them, but I didn't see onions or garlic."

She blinked as if she had no idea how to respond. Instead, she lifted the fork and took a bite. With a thoughtful expression, she chewed and flashed me a quick smile. Everything about the moment felt wrong, but I couldn't put my finger on why.

"It's so good," she said, but I saw she was struggling to swallow.

"If it's not, that's okay, you won't hurt my feelings if you don't want to eat it." Something was going on, but she didn't seem eager to level with me and tell me what it was.

"I noticed your shot glass rack," I teased, trying to lighten the mood. I gestured to the device, and her gaze flicked toward it, and then swept back to me. "I'm not sure if we need to talk about your drinking problem or buy you glasses to fill it."

A second passed, then she let out a nervous laugh.

I tried to figure out what I was missing, but she avoided my eyes, put her fork down, and picked up her coffee.

"It's hot," I warned again, but she took a quick sip anyway. She smiled through gritted teeth.

"Yep, too hot." She exhaled and set the mug back down next to her plate. "Might need a new tongue."

"I burned mine too," I said with a smile.

She stared through me, deep in thought. I promised myself I'd get to the bottom of this.

CHAPTER SIXTEEN

KANDRA

Sucking in a slow breath between my teeth, I tried to cool off my scalding tongue. The liquid lava stung all the way down my throat until it hit my violently roiling belly. I tried to stare past my confusion and guilt and swallow the pain, but it was no use. Blinking away tears, I needed to figure out how to survive the moment.

Noah had made me breakfast and a delicious breakfast at that. The guy could cook, but my stomach was always tied up in knots first thing in the morning. I'd given up big morning meals in favor of dry toast and water, but he didn't know that because I stupidly hadn't told him I was pregnant. Any other time, I'd appreciate this sweet gesture, but as he sat there and smiled at me, I flashed him a grin and tried to figure a way out of this mess.

His hand covered mine on the table, and I glanced down at the touch, then back up to meet his suddenly worried expression. "Is everything all right? You seem off this morning."

I wanted nothing more than to tell him the whole truth, but as my mouth flooded with saliva, I knew if I opened it, my insides would purge. Swallowing hard, I reasoned with my body that it was just an omelet, no reason to freak out. Not that reasoning with morning sickness had ever worked in the past because it hadn't.

My hands started to shake, and my stomach turned wildly. I begged my body not to get sick. Just one day off, I just needed one day without throwing up. I hadn't thought about the potential of this happening last night. What happened between us was incredible and beautiful, but I hadn't even considered what might happen this morning when we woke up. Of course, he wouldn't sneak out. That's not the kind of guy Noah was.

"You're shaking." The concern in his voice covered me like a warm blanket as the sickness eased.

"That coffee sure is hot," I said, trying to cover for everything. Something in me screamed to tell him the truth, but I wasn't sure I could say the words and keep my stomach in check.

Noah nodded, but his troubled expression didn't change as he studied my face.

Where did I start? The lack of onions and garlic because both made me so sick I couldn't eat if they were even in the house? The shot glass rack that was actually a drying rack for baby bottles? How did I explain myself?

Oh, yeah, so I didn't tell you that I'm pregnant with my ex's baby, but thanks for the wonderful sex, and that's not a shot glass rack, it's for baby bottles.

He would hate me, and rightfully so, but I needed to tell him because it was the right thing to do. The last thing I wanted was to hurt him because I had been dishonest.

I took another bite of eggs and instantly regretted it. The second the feta hit my tongue, my stomach twisted, and I couldn't force myself to swallow the bite.

"Did I mess it up?" He looked so anxious, and it made me feel worse about everything. I knew he was afraid he screwed up the food, but the problem wasn't the delicious omelet; it was my lies.

I shook my head as he pulled his hand away and set his coffee mug on the table. Chewing more on the bite, I pushed it to the back of my throat, narrowly missing the gag reflex, and managed to swallow. "You didn't make yourself anything?" I asked before pushing the plate toward him. "It's delicious."

He glanced at it, then at me. "You barely ate." The look of suspicion in his eyes killed me because he had every right to be skeptical, but I had no idea how to confess. That was the problem with lies. They grew because each lie I told required another to cover it up.

"I don't really do breakfast much anymore." I could comfort myself because what I said was the truth, but I knew I wasn't telling him the whole truth, either. Was telling a partial truth just as bad as an outright lie? I had to hope not.

He seemed to accept my reason and took a bite of the omelet while I made my way to the fridge for a glass of milk. Maybe that would help calm the storm in my gut. While I sipped the milk, I struggled with myself. No more putting it off, no more BS. I needed to come clean and just say it. How hard could it be?

Hey, Noah, I'm pregnant. Sorry I didn't tell you before.

Easy-peasy, but as I turned toward him, I saw the slight smile on his face and the warmth in his eyes and thought about last night. Would I ruin everything by confessing now? Was it too late? The thoughts swirled through my brain. Logic said he deserved to know, especially before getting into anything akin to a relationship with me. Even if we were just friends with benefits, shouldn't he be entitled to full disclosure?

"I guess there's a lot I don't know about you anymore. Sorry that I assumed." His expression told me he wanted to learn everything about me, all the new details, all the things that had changed over the years, and my heart melted like butter in the microwave.

"Don't apologize." I was the one that should have been apologizing. I put my empty glass in the sink and walked back to the table to sit opposite him again. The milk seemed to ease the sour in my stomach, and I breathed an internal sigh of relief. That was one crisis averted.

I sat down and smiled. "I appreciate that you made me breakfast. It's one of those sweet gestures I've missed." My ex had never been so sweet. He hadn't been a jerk either, until the end, but he'd never been attentive to small details.

"I'm glad you're back." With the empty fork in his hand pointed down at the plate and his attention on me, I remembered how it had felt before to be the center of his world. I'd loved that feeling; it was like a drug, addictive and thrilling, and that sensation had very nearly stopped me from walking away back then—almost.

"I'm glad to be back." Being here with him was so natural, and last night seemed right. We fit perfectly together, like a lock and key. I didn't quite know what to do next. Well, I knew what I needed to do, but as I opened my mouth, the words weren't there. Instead, a little hiccup escaped me, and I held my breath for a second.

"Are you going to be sick?"

I gave my head a little shake. I wasn't getting sick—I couldn't get sick. That would raise questions, but even as I thought about the reasons I couldn't get sick, bile raced up my throat.

The trembling returned, and my body slicked with an instant, sudden sweat that told me I couldn't deny it any longer. I was going to throw up and nothing, not milk, not holding my breath, and not breathing would stop it. As sweat beaded across my brow, I stood.

He bolted out of his chair, his hands reaching for me. "Are you going to pass out?"

I couldn't focus on what he was saying or an answer to his question. I bolted toward the bathroom at lightning speed, all fear of what he might think of me, how this might play out, or what would happen after this moment left my head as I raced to stand over the toilet.

My stomach coiled, then heaved so hard I couldn't hold back. Fingers gently scraped my hair back from my hot, sticky neck, and Noah's hand found my hip as my stomach lurched, and everything I'd eaten exited.

Miserable, trembling, and weak, his hand steadied me, and I could hear him speaking softly, even though I had no idea what he said.

As the pain in my stomach subsided, and nausea eased up, I waited to see if it was over.

"Well, damn, I guess I need to work on my cooking." Despite the easy humor in his tone, I heard the worry there too.

I couldn't hold back a sharp laugh because I had to find the humor in something.

"Are you pregnant?" His joking comment came right as my stomach tensed again. It would have been funny timing if throwing up didn't make me feel so miserable. Still, he held on to me, offering comfort even as my insides purged.

Everything seemed to calm down again, and I took several deep breaths. The shaking ceased, and the sick, sweaty feeling passed.

I knew from experience that all it took was clearing my stomach, and I'd be fine until the next morning. Well, fine as far as throwing up. Whether or not I'd be fine when I faced Noah was a different story.

"I'm better." I spit the last bit of sourness out before flushing away the evidence. "I need to brush my teeth."

"Okay." He backed off a few steps, but stood in the bathroom doorway, arms crossed, watching me as I put toothpaste on the brush while carefully avoiding his stare.

My upset stomach was gone, and the trembling stopped. I felt fine, but sooner or later, he would ask me what the heck was going on. I mean, everybody knows what morning sickness is, right? How could he not know at this point? Unless he really thought it was his cooking, but I doubted he did. After all, he finished the omelet, and he was fine.

If he asked if I was pregnant again, I'd blurt out, "Yes."

As the minty flavor of toothpaste washed away every trace of bitterness in my mouth, I wished I could just say it now. Why was it so hard? How come it seemed like something stopped me every time I tried to tell him?

With a sparkling clean mouth, I rinsed the brush, turned off the water, and spun to meet his gaze.

Instead of judgment and anger in his features, I saw affection. Warmth. Worry. Compassion. Before I could say anything, he opened his arms, and without thinking, I rushed into them. My heart pounded as I wondered if he knew or was simply being Noah; kind, sweet, thoughtful, loving Noah. He hugged me tightly, and I squeezed my eyes closed and enjoyed being held while he gently played with my hair and pressed his lips to my forehead.

CHAPTER SEVENTEEN

NOAH

I'd never dreaded Saturday dinner at Mom's before.

"Are you two gonna get married?" Quinn swooped into the kitchen behind me.

"Shut up, Quinn." I continued peeling potatoes while he moved toward the sink with a colander of salad greens.

"It's a fair question." Ethan's voice came from behind. "We should know if you're going to elope."

"I vote for Dave to take his spot when he's too whipped to come out with us after work." Quinn made a whip-cracking noise, and I flipped him off before getting back to the task at hand.

"Dave? I thought Paul would be a better fit." Ethan sounded genuinely surprised.

"Great, guys, talk about me like I'm not here. I'm not getting married, and I'm not whipped. Clearly, if you pick someone to replace me, it's Greg." No contest, Greg would be the perfect stand-in for me at the table.

"Greg…" Both of my brothers said his name as if suddenly seeing the light while Bayden made a low sound that told us he wasn't enjoying the conversation.

"What's eating you, brother?" I asked Bayden.

"Not the same person eating you." Quinn moved past me, shaking excess water from the colander on my head. He hurried off when I turned his way, knife in one hand, potato in the other.

He tilted his head, a goofy grin on his face. "You're scarier with a potato, just so you know."

"I could kill you with a potato," I said before glancing at Bayden again. "Anybody know what's up with him?" I asked in a lower voice as he left the kitchen.

"Maybe he has the Angie itch? Or is it Miranda?" Quinn's joke earned him a disgusted grunt from Ethan. We returned to our stations and continued getting dinner ready for Mom.

For a long time, she'd made these dinners, but several years back, we'd decided she worked too hard during the week to also have to make our Saturday family dinner, so we took over. We started simply enough by helping in the kitchen. Within a month, we booted her out, and now we made family dinner for her. That's what being a family was; everyone taking care of each other, not having Mom take care of everything while we did nothing.

This week, Quinn made the salad, Ethan made homemade mac and cheese, and I made mashed potatoes. Bayden was in charge of a slow-cooked brisket he started at home. He'd take the meat juices and make a gravy out of it for my potatoes if I didn't beat him to it. Comfort food, the things Mom made us when we were kids. This close to the anniversary of Dad's passing, we all needed comfort.

"Have you guys … you know?" Quinn's question made me want to punch him in the face.

"Why do you want to know that, you weirdo?" Ethan asked, finally taking my side on something.

I wanted to thank him but had a feeling he wanted to know too.

Quinn shrugged. "I don't. I just want to see how mad I can

make him. I mean, this is Kandra. It's momentous. Our little boy has grown up and found a woman." He draped his arms around my shoulders in a hug, and I shrugged him off.

"Noah met a woman?" Mom's voice filled the kitchen, and both my brothers tensed.

"I, uh, have to use the restroom." Ethan's eyes moved from me to Mom and back again before he slipped out the door toward the hallway.

Quinn stood frozen in place as if standing still would make him invisible to our mother. She crossed her arms and looked at both of us.

Quinn inched sideways. "I'll let him tell you about it." With that, he rushed out of the kitchen while I glared at his retreating back.

In the empty kitchen with my mother, I tried to think my way out of the situation like a young boy might consider talking his way out of having taken a cookie without permission.

She studied me carefully; her expression filled with warmth, love, and understanding. But I knew she remembered how hurt I'd been when Kandra left. I swore then that I'd never let her hurt me like that again, and yet, here I was, acting the fool for her.

But it was different this time, wasn't it? We were adults and had grown as people do when they mature. This time I'd be more careful to guard myself against her leaving.

"Not really," I said, and it was mostly true. I didn't meet a woman. I'd known Kandra for a long time, but I wasn't ready to discuss this with Mom because she'd want answers, and I didn't have them.

Hell, I wasn't ready to discuss it with anyone for that matter, not that that stopped my brothers from tormenting me every chance they got. I couldn't blame them because we all messed with each other, and I knew they cared about me even if they annoyed the shit out of me.

I turned back to the potatoes. As I peeled the last one, Mom gathered the others into a stainless steel mixing bowl and carried them to the sink. The water running into the bowl as she rinsed them made me want to remind her that this was my task—not that she'd let me bully her out of the kitchen.

I moved to her side and dropped the last potato into the bowl. Giving her a one-armed hug around the shoulders, I gently nudged her with a bump of my hip, and she stepped aside while I took the bowl from her. As the water filled the bowl and overflowed into the sink, I waited for her to say something—anything.

Instead, she stayed quiet and moved back to the counter, took out a cutting board and knife, and set them out for me. With the rinsed potato bowl in hand, I carried it over toward the cutting board while waiting for the other shoe to drop.

"Does this have something to do with Kandra being back in town?" Her quiet question hit me like a dart. Every muscle in my body tightened. I wasn't eager to have this conversation.

I carefully cubed potatoes and put them into the stockpot. What could I say? I wouldn't lie to my mother, but how could I explain our relationship when I didn't understand it myself?

"It's complicated." That was the best explanation I could muster. I shifted, hating being put on the spot. I silently reminded myself to make sure to put Quinn in the hot seat the first chance I got.

"Are you thinking about seeing her again?" Mom leaned against the counter next to me as I carefully sliced through a halved potato.

I sighed. "I don't want to talk about this right now. Like I said, it's complicated."

To my surprise, she didn't ask any more questions. Instead, she wound her arms around me. "I love you and matters of the heart are always complicated." She rose on tiptoes and pressed a kiss to my cheek before leaving the room while calling out for Quinn in her *you're in trouble, mister* voice.

I sighed and leaned against the counter. Maybe it should have been confusing or difficult, but it wasn't. Being with Kandra felt right. Perhaps it was stupid to jump back in given our past, but I wanted to trust that things would be different, that we could make us work.

Was that such a far-fetched idea?

WITH THE TABLE ready and all the delicious comfort foods set out, we took our seats.

I glanced at Dad's spot as memories of him laughing at one of our terrible jokes came to mind. Memories of him talking to us about our day. His gentle approval at our good grades; his disproval of Bayden getting into a fight. Though he agreed Bayden did the right thing by standing up for himself, he'd also said he wished my brother could have resolved the issue without violence, but he'd been quick to say he understood not everything could be easily solved.

My moment of silence went unbroken, and I realized everyone was thinking about him. Quinn spoke up first. "Remember that time he made a mask out of a paper plate and tried to scare us with it?"

I remembered the diversionary *look over there* he'd done that made us all look away, and when we glanced back, he had a painted paper plate covering his face. Quinn had jumped, but the rest of us laughed.

"Yeah, he scared you." Ethan's voice held a hint of humor and an edge of agony and loss.

We'd talked about the girls we liked, the philosophy of life, and everything big and small. Dinner was forever quieter without him.

Mom's eyes misted over, and she blinked while staring straight ahead. Her hands balled up on either side of her plate, and she seemed to be looking past us at something we couldn't see. Without thinking about it, I stood up and walked over to her. Winding my arms around her, I spoke softly. "I love you."

She patted my arm. "I love you, too."

A moment later, Quinn's arms came around her, and Ethan followed suit. Bayden covered her hand with his, and we hugged as a group.

She let out a light sniff and a little laugh. "I think I heard your stomach growl." She looked at Quinn. "Let's eat before the food gets cold. It looks and smells delicious."

We broke apart and retook our spots. As we passed food around the table and loaded up our plates, Quinn started in on Bayden. I breathed a sigh of relief that he was off my back for now, though, I felt bad for Bayden.

"Have you asked her out yet?" Quinn elbowed Bayden, who shrugged him off and took a bite of mac and cheese.

"Has he asked who out?" Mom watched both her sons closely while I dumped gravy on my potatoes and noticed the sparkle in Ethan's eyes.

Quinn continued to stare at Bayden while he answered our mother. "He's in love with the new sheriff."

"I'm not in love with her." Bayden elbowed Quinn in the ribs, and his twin let out a pained exhale.

It didn't even slow him down. "Oh, no? You let her walk around on the job site." Quinn grinned, and I found I wasn't the only one who noticed that out of character move. Bayden was safety-minded and didn't let anyone walk around our construction sites.

"We're building the new police station. It's not that weird to let Miranda tour it." Bayden shoved a bite of mashed potato into his mouth, though his sullen expression told everyone he knew they were onto him. His gaze slid to me, and he quickly swallowed.

"Besides, weren't we talking about how he and Kandra are back together?"

Quinn froze, Ethan stopped chewing, and Mom's head swiveled in my direction. Bayden's eyebrows lifted as if he only just realized he'd called me out in front of Mom. His silent apology didn't save me from the spotlight, though, and I wiped my mouth calmly with my napkin, took a sip of my water, and casually picked up another bite of food.

"We're not together, but it's interesting how desperate you are to deflect attention away from you and the new sheriff, especially with how hard you stare at her every time she comes to Roy's."

Quinn sucked in a deep breath as his smile broadened, and Bayden's eyes narrowed. I shoved the bite of mac and cheese into my mouth. *Get out of that, Bayden.*

CHAPTER EIGHTEEN

KANDRA

My phone rang, and I raced into my room to grab it off the bedside table. "Hello?"

I'd been wandering around the nursery trying to wrap my head around this whole pregnancy thing. I was going to be a mom. Sometimes it just struck me, and I couldn't hold back a smile.

"Good morning." Noah's deep voice filled my ear, and I sighed.

"Is it still morning?" I teased.

"It's eleven." His humorous, slightly defensive tone made me laugh. "But I waited until it was this late to call you. I wanted to see if you'd have lunch with me, or maybe we could grab a beer?"

I giggled, totally ready to turn his words back on him. "It's eleven in the morning, who has a drinking problem now?"

"Oh, look at you being all judgy." He chuckled on the other end, but I could sense he was waiting for my response.

"I'd love to go to brunch with you." As I said the words, something occurred to me. "Wait, is this a date?"

"Well, I guess it is."

"Although I just realized I have something to do at one." I

thought about Max's gift. I'd done all the legwork to make sure it would be safe, but I worried our brunch could run long.

"Are you blowing me off?" He didn't sound mad, merely curious.

"No, but I have this coupon a friend gave me to go riding."

A second ticked by. "Does this friend happen to be Max?"

How did he know? "Actually, yes, why?"

"Because he got me the same thing, and I have a ride scheduled for today at one too." His dry tone didn't hint to his thoughts, but as it sank in, I remembered the way Max had spoken to me, and the thoughtful gift he'd given. It was for the same barn where I had my thirteenth birthday party, and all the beautiful memories tied to the place came rushing back when I opened the gift.

"He tried to parent-trap us." I breathed the words as tears tickled my eyes. It was so sweet and devious of him. "Want to go do that, then grab a bite to eat?"

"Sure. I can't believe Max. He knew it would force us to spend time together if we were too stubborn to admit our feelings for each other, or it would end up being a date." He laughed on the other end of the line, and I enjoyed the sound.

"I wondered why it was a private ride. Now I know it's because it's just supposed to be for the two of us." I needed to thank Max next time I saw him. "If we're going together, I need to get ready."

"I'll call and see if we can show up early."

"Oh, Margie will be fine with that, if she's still running the place." Margie was a fantastic old cowpoke of a woman, tough as nails and gritty as they come. She'd have been right at home in the wild west alongside the cowboys, though I bet she could outride, outshoot, and outspit them any day.

"I'll double-check." With that, he was gone, and I smiled all the way to the bathroom.

I hadn't ridden a horse in so many years, and I'd taken the time to do a ton of research to make sure it was something I could do pregnant. Everything seemed safe, as long as I didn't fall. I was confident that riding a horse was like riding a bike—you didn't forget. We weren't going to do anything extreme. Likely, it was just a trail ride, which was slow and safe.

WE RODE past a house on the creek where we played as kids. The Crafts had owned the property for as long as I could remember. Mark Craft had been a buddy of Noah's and always invited him to hang out. "Do you remember tossing me in the creek?"

"Yep. I also remember you getting me back and pulling me in when I tried to help you out."

I laughed. "It was only fair. If I was getting wet, so were you."

"It took me ten years, but I got you back."

I knew he was talking about the showerhead fiasco that wasn't a disaster after all because it was a step in getting us back together.

As we passed the house, I noticed the realtor's sign in the window. "I can't believe the Crafts sold the place."

Noah turned his horse, and we headed back the way we came. Our hour was almost up. "They got older and couldn't keep up with the house. Besides, Mark got married and had a baby, and they went to stay with him in California to be closer to their grandchild."

The vacant house pulled at my heart. So many sacrifices were made for love. "It was a great house to raise a kid in. Hopefully, a nice family will buy it and fix it up."

"It definitely needs a lot of work, but you're right, it would be great to see it brought back to life." He looked over his shoulder as we moved farther away. "This is a playground for kids with the creek, the treehouse, and the large yard."

My stomach growled. "Race you back to the stables. I'm starving."

Noah didn't need my challenge. He took off like a bee running from a swatter while I cantered back to the stables. As soon as we turned in our horses, we headed straight for the diner.

Once in the parking lot, Noah raced to my side and picked me up out of his truck. I laughed as he cradled me to his chest outside the diner. This was part of what I missed about being with him. Noah never skimped on affection.

"Thank you for going with me. It was fun." I looked into his eyes, and my heart beat a little too fast. I was falling in love with Noah all over again. The boy had grown into a man, and I was sure we'd grown into each other, not out of each other.

"Are you ready to eat?" he asked, gently setting me on my feet.

I nodded. "I've got a hankering for fluffy waffles with whipped cream and strawberries drowning in blueberry syrup."

He stared at me for a second. "You're walking into Dottie's, home of the most famous pancakes this side of the world, and you're ordering waffles?"

"You can pretend you don't know me," I joked, slipping my hand in his as we walked toward the door.

"I might have to," he muttered, laughter in his eyes.

As we made our way to the entrance, I realized I didn't care if the town gossip saw us holding hands. I didn't care if the world knew Noah and I were together again. The only thing I considered was making sure I told him the truth. By the end of our date, Noah would finally know I was pregnant.

I hoped there would be an easy way to do it. That there would be some natural way to ease it into the conversation. I could apologize for not saying anything. Maybe if he knew I wasn't telling anyone, not even my mom, it would make a difference. Hopefully, he wouldn't be mad if he knew I wasn't hiding it only from him.

He squeezed my hand. "You seem lost in thought." We

stopped in front of the door, and he gently turned me to face him. "Are you okay? Feeling sick?"

I shook my head. "No, not feeling sick, but we do need to talk." *Way to ease in, Kandra.*

"Oh, we will talk—over pancakes." He opened the door and motioned me inside; no hint of worry or concern at my ominous words.

"I'm getting waffles," I said over my shoulder as I stepped inside and headed for a table by a window that looked out at the mountains. The dark-green trees and pretty view set the tone as Noah joined me.

He chuckled as Dottie came rushing over. "Hey kids," she said, her smile on high beam as she hovered.

"Hi, Dottie. I'd like pancakes, please." He eyed me as if he could mad dog me into getting pancakes, and I laughed. I loved his easy humor and his hardline stance on my choice of breakfast food, though I knew it was all in fun.

"I'd like waffles with whipped cream, strawberries, and blueberry syrup, please."

She nodded. "And to drink?"

"He probably wants a beer, he has been talking about it since breakfast," I said quickly before asking for a Sprite. I avoided his stare and tried not to laugh at Dottie's expression. Clearly, she knew I was poking fun at him.

"ID please?"

His eyes widened. "Are you kidding?"

She nodded her head and tapped him with the order pad. "You know we don't serve spirits here. You'll have to go to Roy's if a beer is what you want."

"I'd actually like a coffee, black and bottomless, please."

Dottie glanced at me. "You need to have a conversation with this young man about his drinking problem."

"Oh, I will." I laughed as she walked off, and Noah stared at me.

"What just happened?" he asked, sounding perplexed.

"I ordered waffles, and you nearly showed her your ID for coffee." I planted my elbows on the table and tucked my hands under my chin as Dottie hurried back with his coffee and my Sprite and left again.

"Are you still feeling sick?" he asked me.

Tell him now! Despite my brain screaming directions, when his eyes focused on me, I couldn't say the words. I wanted this to be a nice meal. I'd wait until the end, but I would tell him. When we have finished eating and the odds of making a scene were the lowest, I'd spill the beans.

"Off and on. How is the new project you're working on?" I'd seen his construction crew building something in town, though I wasn't sure what it was.

"The new police station is going well." He seemed pleased that I asked.

"I'd love to listen to you talk about work at some point." How they created buildings from bare patches of land and lumber fascinated me.

His expression lit up. "I'd like that," he said, picking up his coffee. "How's it going at Roy's?"

"I like it." I thought working in a bar would be uncomfortable, and it would have been anywhere else, but everyone that came into Roy's was more like family than anything. It felt like home. "Roy is a great boss."

Noah nodded. "Yeah, he's a good man, and I'm glad you like it there. It's nice to have another friendly face around, and Roy needs help."

I was glad he didn't think I shouldn't be working at a bar. "Thank you for doing this." I put my hand over his, and our eyes met across the table.

"For doing what?"

"Coming out with me. I've had so much fun with you today. I'm glad to have you in my life again. I just wish we never had to spend so many years apart. I know that was my fault, but I will never stop trying to make it up to you." The words poured out without a filter, and I could only hope I wouldn't scare him away. Judging by the warmth in his eyes, he felt the same way.

"It has been my pleasure spending the day with you. And you don't have to make anything up to me, I have forgiven you already, and you are here with me now, where you belong. Since the day you left, I never wanted anyone else, and now that you're back, I know it is because you were always the one I wanted to be with." His eyes shifted between mine as his meaning sunk in.

My spongy heart soaked up his words. "You're the one I want to be with, too."

I leaned forward across the table and grabbed the back of his head. Pressing my lips to his, not caring who saw.

He let out a soft growl, and his tongue slid along my lower lip, where he nipped at it. Excitement thundered through my veins, and I wanted more. Instead, I pulled back, because we were in a public place. Unable to catch my breath, I studied his expression. The hunger there echoed my arousal.

"I'm glad we're giving us another try," I whispered the words, and he nodded, leaning in close enough to press his forehead to mine.

"Me too. It feels right."

Everything was okay in the world because I could do anything with Noah by my side.

CHAPTER NINETEEN

NOAH

Her expression shifted to one of annoyance as she glanced over my shoulder. She quickly ducked her head, keeping my body between her and whoever she was trying to avoid.

Dottie walked over with her waffles and my pancakes and refilled my coffee. The second she was gone, I glanced at Kandra.

"Were you hiding from Dottie?"

Her gaze slid to mine as she slumped further in her chair and continued hunkering down. "No." Picking up her fork, she nipped a bit of whipped cream and a cut strawberry and popped the sweet bite into her mouth before dumping syrup all over the mess.

"Who, then?" I didn't want to glance over my shoulder and make her more obvious to whoever she was hiding from, but as the seconds ticked by, her discomfort seeped into me and lined my gut with a frost-like chill.

Before she could answer, I heard Benji's voice. "Kandra?"

He was straight-up shouting at her across the diner. The smattering of other people there began to murmur. The sounds of backsides shifting in chairs and throat-clearing told me things were about to escalate into a full-blown public scene.

Kandra flinched at her name on his lips, and fear filled her eyes. I swallowed back my rage and stood up, turning to face Benji. His tweed jacket, bright-yellow tie, and lime-green shirt assaulted my eyes, and I wanted to hit him based solely on his clothing.

With his head down and a maniacal gleam glaring past me, he put me on edge. He marched right up like he was on the warpath. I sidestepped to block him from Kandra.

Benji danced around me to glower at her, so I put an arm out to block him, and he shoved it away. My fist balled up, and Kandra's panicked voice rang in my ears.

"Noah, it's okay." Her tone told me it was not okay, and the need to beat down this little shit intimidating her overwhelmed me. I grabbed Benji's collar and hauled him back a few feet while his arms windmilled and furious gibberish sputtered from his lips like bubbles from a drowning man.

"Stay back, or I'll drag you outside, and we'll settle this like men. Give her space." If this was happening, Benji would need to be respectful and not try to intimidate her.

Still, he ignored me and continued to glare at Kandra.

She finally looked at him, taking a slow, labored breath and appearing oddly pale.

"What, Benji?" Her voice was barely a whisper.

Benji puffed up and squared his shoulders, leaning forward with a strange light in his eyes.

I waited with every muscle and tendon in my body taut and ready to spring into action if he so much as breathed in her direction the wrong way.

Kandra stopped looking at him and drew in her whipped cream with her fork's tines, though the fluffy white mound had mostly melted into the waffle. Her hand trembled slightly, and she set the fork down to take a sip of her Sprite. Nothing she did seemed to ease the genuine fear she appeared to be experiencing, and I wondered what I'd missed. What happened between these two to make her so afraid of Benji?

"I wanted to do a story on your return for the paper." Benji's tone held a note of sick glee, and Kandra froze, but Benji pressed on. "It will be a welcome back kind of article. The prodigal daughter returns after conquering the modeling world."

I somehow doubted it was anything like that because Benji liked to destroy people he thought had wronged him somehow. I had no doubts he'd write an exposé of some sort on Sherriff Miranda after her constant refusal to give him the time of day.

The guy had always been a sleaze-bag.

"That's very nice of you." Kandra's voice sounded strangled, and I knew she was waiting for him to deliver whatever blow he had locked and loaded for her.

Benji nodded. "I like for the town to stay informed of everything that's going on."

Kandra nodded, her somber mood not lifting one bit. "Yep, small-town news. Nothing big happens, so you have to air people's dirty laundry or transgressions you think you've found."

I wanted to applaud her cutting words, but instead, I held back. She wanted to go toe-to-toe with this guy, so I'd only step in if she wanted or needed me. I knew she could handle herself just fine.

Benji's cheeks went bright red. The color clashed with his hideous outfit, somehow. "Things happen here, and people have a right to know." His livid response almost earned a laugh from me.

"Yep, the Prestons' cat had five kittens. The Lockhart brothers are making great progress on the new police station, but are they overcharging the city?" she said. "Nope, it turns out they're not. Will the pothole on Main Street ever be filled? Residents demand answers." She took another sip of her soda, and I couldn't hold back a snide grin. She'd just word-for-word recited several of the headlines he'd put out over the last month.

"Make fun of me all you want. I learned some things about what you were up to while you were gone." He crossed his arms.

"I'm not making fun of you." She set her soda down and studied the ring of water on the table.

Benji wasn't done talking. "Your ex sure had a lot to say."

She flinched like he'd hit her. Her head snapped up, and she stared at him. Her mouth opened like she was about to ask him what he was talking about, but the light dawning in her eyes told me she knew exactly what he was about to say.

I prepared for Benji to fling false allegations from her ex. The guy was a hack, a predator, and I'd been saying so from day one. What could he have said to make her look bad? Maybe she did some nude photoshoots or something? I could imagine her not wanting that to get out in today's climate, but that was on him as her manager, not her as the model. It wouldn't sway my opinion of her in any way. Even if she did nude photoshoots, I didn't give a damn, because it wasn't my place to judge her past.

What could the idiot possibly have said to Benji that could have her looking so pale? I couldn't think of anything.

"Please don't." She didn't seem to know what to say, and her words sounded like she was begging him not to say whatever he was about to.

I stepped toward him, ready to escort him outside as roughly as I could without it becoming an assault charge, but Kandra lifted a hand to stop me. "Noah, please."

She stared at Benji, who glanced from her to me and back again.

"Please don't do this." Her tone took on an exhausted edge, as if she was so bitterly tired she couldn't come up with any other words. "Not here. We can talk in private if needed."

The second those words left her lips, my hackles rose. Under no circumstances did I want Benji alone with Kandra because I didn't trust him. He leveraged some silent threat against her in front of me. What would he do if he got her alone?

Benji hesitated as if considering her offer, and then, all of a sudden, he seemed to deflate. It was as if he knew what she was offering wouldn't wind up being what he wanted, and a malicious look crossed his face.

It was a look I recognized. A look that said *if I can't have you, nobody can.*

It was apparent he was out to destroy her. Whatever he had on her was bad—bad enough to devastate her.

Benji looked at me, his evil little eyes studying my face. He seemed satisfied that he knew more than me, and his ugly smirk turned smug as his attention returned to Kandra. "He doesn't know, does he?"

Finding myself suddenly in the middle of this oddly tense conversation, I glanced at Kandra. Her eyes were locked on Benji, and I could see the silent plea in her expression and the fear across her face. She swallowed hard as if she was about to be sick.

The diner was silent with people pretending not to listen while hanging on every word, and I knew Kandra's hatred for confrontation was likely adding to her stress.

"Look, whatever she hasn't told me isn't my business. She'll tell me when she's ready." I lifted my shoulders, feeling pretty blasé about the whole threat. "Or she won't."

Benji laughed. A real, throw your head back, hold your stomach laugh that brought me right back to wanting to deck him.

He glanced at me when he calmed down and wiped a stray tear from the corner of his eye. "Oh, that's precious." He pointed between the two of us and swung his index finger back and forth like a pendulum. "I take it you're a couple, right? That's the rumor, anyhow."

"That's none of your damn business." Neither of us owed him an explanation.

"Oh, no need to get all defensive with me. I already know everything I need to know to keep the hell away from her." He said the words with such disdain, I lifted my fist a few inches.

Kandra grabbed my wrist, and I relaxed a little bit.

"Yes, we all know you're a big, strong man." Benji rolled his eyes. "A big, strong man that deserves to know that his girlfriend is keeping something from you."

He was toying with me, and I wasn't in the mood. "Don't you have some garbage news story to cover? Pretty sure tweed went out of fashion forty years ago. Maybe you can do something with that."

He tugged his lapels and rolled his neck. "I'm wounded. Aren't you curious?"

I was, but I stood by what I'd said; she would tell me when she was ready. I had no right to demand or expect information from her.

"Not really. Not sure I'd trust it from you anyway. Does she know the real reason you pretended to be her friend all those years?" I took a step closer to him even as Kandra tried to hold me back. "Does she know you only wanted one thing from her? It seems pretty suspect now that you've discovered she won't give you the time of day, you try to ruin her life with what … a secret that's hers to keep?"

He planted his hands on my shoulders. "Noah, my friend … she's pregnant."

CHAPTER TWENTY

KANDRA

Noah looked like he'd been punched in the stomach as Benji's hands fell from his shoulders. I stood there, unable to breathe. Asphyxiation might have been preferable to that moment. As Benji turned to me, the satisfaction in his eyes sickened my stomach.

"Were you planning to dupe Noah here into thinking he was the daddy?" He couldn't hold back a smug grin as he stared at me.

I blinked and resisted the urge to slap the smile right off his stupid face. Instead, I shook my head. "What is wrong with you?" I asked. Truly stunned that anyone would even think I could do something like that, I shifted uneasily. Did Noah believe that's what I was trying to do?

"What's wrong with me? Honey, you're the one who hid this pregnancy from everyone, even your boyfriend. What do you think people will believe?" He crossed his arms and studied me like he thought I would answer. Like he thought I owed him an answer.

I glanced at Noah and noticed his jaw flexing. I wanted to talk to him, but I didn't know how to get rid of Benji.

"This exposé will be great for sales." Benji pulled my attention back, and the way he gleefully rubbed his hands together made my stomach twist. He faked concern as he glanced at me. "It might not be so good for you, though." The forced frown on his lips didn't hide the joy in his expression.

My brows knitted together as pure hatred filled me. "Shame on you, Benji. The news was mine to distribute. This is the twenty-first century, and I have no obligation to share this kind of thing with anyone. You plan to tell the world without my permission in order to try to shame me, and that's disgusting."

I lifted my chin and took a step closer. His eyes widened, and I continued talking. "You're reprehensible. It says a lot about your character when you're so desperate to sell papers you don't care if you become a tabloid. Congratulations because nobody will ever take you seriously as a journalist. Might as well sign up for some celebrity watch rag."

My words seemed to ruffle him, and he glanced at Noah, back at me, and then around the diner. I took in people's glares and ducked my head. I hated being humiliated in public. I'd never forgive Benji for this.

"Some friend you are," I whispered. To my horror, my eyes filled with stinging hot tears. Noah was right; Benji was never my friend, but more accurately, my enemy. Maybe I'd always known it. He always seemed less concerned about me and more interested in being *with* me.

I was wrong.

Noah still hadn't said a word, and he wasn't looking at me either. I wanted to talk to him to repair the damage before it was too late, but Benji didn't seem ready to leave me alone.

"You can go now," I told him. "You got what you wanted. You embarrassed me, messed up my relationship with the man I love, and you stole the opportunity from me to tell my news when I was ready."

Benji chuckled, but the fire seemed to have left his eyes. Someone in the diner cleared their throat, and the harsh sound made Benji jump. He glanced over to see glares aimed in our direction and gave Dottie a weak smile.

She disappeared into the back without acknowledging him.

I couldn't hold back my tears anymore, and two slipped down my cheeks. Furious with myself for crying, I swiped them away.

"You can't make me leave." Benji planted his feet and straightened his shoulders. "Besides, I'd like a statement from the man you were going to pin another man's baby on."

I shook my head. "You can try to twist the narrative all you want. There are plenty of reasons why women don't tell people they're pregnant. Duping someone into being the father isn't one of them. Not for me, at least." There were many reasons for my silence but Noah was never one of them. "It doesn't matter. My reasons for not sharing are my own, and they are valid. You have no business asking questions. Now, leave me alone before I call the cops on you for harassment."

His brows shot up. "I'm not harassing you."

"You're cruel and insulting, and you deliberately hunted me down to do this." I pulled out my phone. "I bet Sheriff Miranda would be interested to hear about this."

That seemed to sway him. He glanced at the table behind me where our food was cold and our date ruined.

"Enjoy your lunch, lovebirds." With that, he shoved his hands into his pockets and sauntered out the door.

My face had to be as hot as the surface of the sun and redder than a tomato. I turned to Noah and saw him tucking money under his plate—more than enough to cover our uneaten meal.

I stepped closer to him and reached for him. "Noah—"

He pulled back without even looking at me.

Fear turned my blood to ice water, and I watched him turn toward the door and walk away without so much as a word or glance. He was just going to step out of my life like nothing had happened between us. This was because I'd screwed up. Because Benji told my secret. Because I'd been too much of a coward to tell him myself.

This mess was all my fault, and I knew it. Still, I had to try to fix this, so I bolted after him, struggling to keep up with his long, swinging stride.

"Noah..." I called after him, but he didn't stop or slow down. "Can we talk about this?" I darted in front of him and walked backward so I could look him in the face.

He refused to look at me. Instead, he stared over my head, his eyes narrowed, and his expression cold and unreadable.

"Can you please give me a chance to explain?" I needed comfort, love, and warmth to help me through the pain and humiliation of what just transpired, but judging by the chill in his icy eyes, I wasn't going to get that from him.

I slowed down, and he walked around me. My heart broke into tiny sharp shards inside my chest. Little blades of glass that cut me until I was sure I'd bleed out.

I watched him go, then followed him to his truck. "Noah, I care about you. I would never try to make you think it was your baby. I wasn't out to trick you."

That seemed to strike a nerve because he turned to me, his expression so dead, a shudder ran through me. "Oh, no?" All the warmth left his voice. "You weren't out to trick me?"

I shook my head.

Anger filled his eyes, and I gasped as he took a step closer. His Adam's apple bobbed as he swallowed.

My natural instinct was to jump back and protect myself.

"Do you think I'd hurt you?"

"Not physically," I said with every bit of raw honesty I possessed.

He hesitated, his gaze wandering over our surroundings before coming back to me. "You slept with me." His low growl of a voice hurt me more than yelling ever could have. "You told me you wanted to be with me, that you wanted to give us another go. I trusted you, but you were lying the whole time, and now you're afraid I will hurt you? Maybe we were never a good match, after all."

Every word cut deeper, and the pain flowed freely from each slice.

"I'm sorry." My eyes filled with fresh tears, and I impatiently blinked them back. I didn't want to freaking cry.

"I should have figured it out when you didn't ask me to wear a condom. I just stupidly thought you were on birth control. Then there was the morning sickness..." he hesitated, likely running through everything in his mind.

"I'm sorry. I planned to tell you today after lunch. I swear."

He stared at me, then snorted. "Convenient. Did it cross your mind that it would be too little, too late?"

It had.

As if he knew there was nothing I could say, he took another step closer, lowering his voice again. "I'm starting to think I dodged a bullet, and maybe I should thank Benji."

He cut me to the bone with those words. Tears flowed freely down my face to dot my shirt.

"Are you breaking up with me?" I whispered, needing to hear him say it. Needing the final nail in the coffin that our relationship would be buried in.

He snorted. "Do you need me to be the bad guy here? Fine. Yes. We're through."

It wasn't that I needed him to be the villain. I just needed to know so I could move on with my life and know there was nothing left between us. I needed that confirmation so I wouldn't wonder *what if* at night.

"I'm not blaming you because I know I did this." My heart

ached, and I turned to walk toward the road, blindly heading toward home. Desperate to get there, I picked up the pace.

"I'll give you a ride. I'm not an asshole."

Despite Noah's words behind me, I didn't want to get in a truck with him. I didn't want the silent, painful, awkward ride home with his scent in my nostrils and memories of how happy we'd been on the way to the diner versus how painful leaving had become.

Ignoring him because I knew I couldn't speak; I continued my trek. A moment later, his truck roared to life, and he pulled beside me. "Let me give you a ride home," he said from the rolled-down window.

I shook my head. "No, thanks." I turned off the road and took a shortcut between buildings so he couldn't follow me. I knew this all had the potential to blow up in my face, but I never expected it to go this badly.

Cutting across the grass, I headed for the footbridge to cross the creek as footfalls warned me that someone was coming up on me fast. I flinched as Noah caught up with me. I stopped walking. "Look, I know I screwed up. You don't have to walk me home. I'll be safe." I couldn't look at him for fear the floodgates would open again.

"Why didn't you tell me?" His quiet voice sent a bolt of pain lancing through my already broken heart.

"I didn't tell anyone. Not even my mom. Just leave me alone, Noah. I won't bother you anymore." With that, I turned toward home.

CHAPTER TWENTY-ONE

NOAH

I glanced at my phone as the ringtone played. It was Mom—again. With the tip of my index finger, I touched the red icon before rolling onto my back and staring at the ceiling.

I'd called into work because I was sick of the lies, the bullshit, and of losing Kandra every time I thought things were going well. The look in her eyes as she told me she wouldn't bother me anymore stuck in my brain. The sheen of tears and the redness in her face haunted me.

Shouldn't I feel furious? She lied to me.

My phone buzzed, notifying me of the hundredth voicemail from Mom.

I turned onto my side and stared at the wall without really seeing it.

Everyone had been trying to get hold of me. Quinn and Mom were neck and neck for the most calls, and I'd been surprised when even Bayden reached out, but I hadn't answered any of them. I sent Quinn a text to let him know I was okay and to leave me alone.

I didn't want to talk. My brothers knew everything. The whole damn town knew everything. Benji had made sure to make a scene in front of Dottie, the town gossip. For such a sweet old lady, she sure didn't know when to keep things to herself. Maybe it wasn't just her, perhaps everyone else who'd been there had been whispering too.

The whole situation was humiliating.

Why hadn't she just told me? Why hide it? I didn't want to think Benji could ever be right about anything, but what if he was? What if she planned to pin it on me? I might have married her and given her the rest of my life. Would I ever have found out if not for Benji?

She told me she planned to come clean at the end of our date, and she seemed genuine. Maybe that was her attempt at damage control?

My phone buzzed again, and I picked it up.

Quinn texted.

Mom's worried about you, and she might call the cops if you don't talk to her.

It's not illegal to be sick. I texted back.

His reply was nearly instant.

But Mom can call in a wellness check to the sheriff's office. Imagine how Bayden will act if Miranda has to come to your place while you're all vulnerable. She won't be able to resist you, and he'll kick your ass.

Not interested in engaging, I put the phone down, but it buzzed again.

Rolling my head to the side, I stared at it but couldn't make out the text at the angle I was at, so a second later, I grabbed it.

Don't underestimate the rebound. I could hear the sarcasm in his text.

Don't you have work to do?

Nope. He replied.

I groaned. When Quinn was on something like this, he never

stopped. There was no getting rid of him now. I'd be better off putting my phone on silent or hiding it in my truck for some peace.

Rolling over again, I stared out the window and wondered what to do next. It was eight a.m., and I tried to sleep in but didn't have much luck with everyone's texts and my mind full of Kandra and her most recent betrayal.

I stood up and grabbed a change of clothes. Might as well grab a shower and pretend to be a functioning human being.

Ten minutes later, I stepped out, clean, and ready to try the next option. Maybe breakfast would help. Once I was dressed, I walked toward my kitchen as a knock at the door vibrated through my home. *Did Mom actually call the cops for a wellness check?*

Adjusting my eye at the peephole, I glanced out into the sunny brightness, and Quinn's face came into view. I considered silently sneaking back to the kitchen and ignoring him.

"I know you're home. Let me in, or I'm coming through the window." His voice made me cringe.

Of course, he knew about the busted kitchen window. I could bluff and claim I'd fixed it, but he'd know I was lying if he called me on it. I could be an ass, but I was never a liar.

I reluctantly opened the front door and let him in. He opened his mouth, and I lifted a hand. "Don't."

"What would Dad have done?"

I wanted to slam the door in his face. "That's how you're going to lead?"

He shrugged and stepped inside. "I've already been talking about it in my head with him for two hours. Sorry if you're behind." He closed the door, and I headed for the kitchen to make breakfast, but he wasn't done talking.

"Dad was the kind of guy that taught us to take care of the people we love."

He was right, but he was a douche for bringing Dad into this. I got coffee brewing and turned to face him.

"You're the one that's most like Dad. You stand for the same things he did. Is this the man you want to be? The man that gets your panties in a twist and hides at home when you find out the woman you love is pregnant?" His earnest tone took some of the sting out of his words.

"Careful," I warned him.

"This isn't you. You're not petty or selfish. You're not the type to run when the going gets tough." He lifted his shoulders as his eyes met mine. "That's not how Dad raised you. It's not how he raised any of us."

"Why aren't you at work?" I didn't want to answer his questions, because I didn't know how to respond. *Would Dad be disappointed in me?*

"I took a personal day." He watched me closely. "You love her, don't you?"

As the smell of coffee flowed through my kitchen, I scanned the room. Taking in the stainless steel appliances, the dark granite countertops, the modern black table and chairs, I sighed. "It doesn't matter if I love Kandra because she hid her pregnancy from me."

"From you, or everybody?" His gentle tone as he took a seat at the table made me hesitate.

"What's the difference?" Did it matter if she hid it from everyone or just from me? Would I feel any better knowing she kept it to herself?

Something about that line of thinking had me shifting uncomfortably. What would Dad have told me? Probably that there are all sorts of reasons people do things.

What reason could be good enough to hide a pregnancy from the guy you're dating?

She told me she hadn't even told her mother. When I closed

my eyes, I saw the horror on her face as Benji outed her news publicly ... she'd been humiliated and scared. *Scared*. Was fear her reason?

"The difference is intent." Quinn had never sounded more like Dad in all his life. "Was her intent to hurt you, or was her intent to protect her privacy?"

He was making far too much sense, especially knowing what I knew about her. Kandra was a private person and often suffered in silence. "She hasn't even told her mom she's pregnant."

Quinn's eyes widened. "And you're still worried this was some nefarious plot against you? Did you ask her why she didn't tell anyone?"

I nodded, then amended the action with words. "I asked her why she didn't tell me."

He shook his head. "You can't make this about you. Did you know the first trimester is the trickiest?" He shrugged. "That's what I read today when I googled why people don't tell others they are pregnant. That thing they call the internet is a marvelous resource. If you have any intention to fix this, then it has to be about her."

Did I want to fix it? "I can't live with someone who keeps secrets like this."

"Did you trust her with everything?" he asked, fixing me with a stare that told me what he was really asking. Initially, I hadn't told her about Dad's death. The timing wasn't right.

I shook my head. "But that's different."

He crossed his arms and sat back. "How so?"

"I didn't want to share. I didn't want her to feel sorry for me. Things had started out rocky when she first got back to town."

My words clicked. I had my reasons for not telling her my father had passed away while she was gone. She had her reasons for not telling me she was pregnant when she got back. Maybe they weren't the same situation, but Dad would have told me to find out the reason first. He'd always been fair, and he said intent meant everything. If her purpose wasn't to deceive me, but to protect herself, could I be mad at her? Was I the asshole?

"I don't know how to make this better." I glanced at Quinn and lifted my shoulders a few inches.

"Start with an apology." Quinn's words brought up my hackles, but before I could speak, he held up a hand. The coffee maker sputtered and hissed, a sure signal it was finished, but I made no move for cups as I stared at my brother.

"She needs support. I can't even imagine what she's going through right now." His words weren't accusatory, but sincere. "Imagine losing your career through no fault of your own, getting knocked up and dumped, then coming home with a secret. Then imagine being publicly humiliated, dumped again, and having a whole town gossiping about you." His gaze met mine, and I knew he was right. "She didn't even tell her family." He stood up and moved toward the cabinet. I watched him grab two mugs and pour the coffee as he gave me the side-eye. "And you made it all about you."

He shook his head and put the mug on the counter. The steel-gray stoneware clinked on the granite, the small sound like a gunshot, and I recoiled. As he filled the second cup, I tried to face the guilt flooding me.

"What would Dad have done?"

He glanced at me. "Well, he wouldn't have broken up with her."

"Thanks." At least he was helpful.

"I think, if it were Mom, he would have done anything to win her back, no matter what it took." Quinn shrugged.

"I don't know how to win her back." I screwed up. In truth, I didn't really give a damn if she was pregnant. The only part of it that bothered me was the secrecy. If I removed my hurt feelings and looked at things objectively, I realized it wasn't about me. It was just like Quinn had said, but I wasn't giving him the satisfaction of saying he was right.

Quinn put a hand on my shoulder and gave me a serious stare. "I wish I could help, but I'm shit with women, and this seems like it needs more than flowers, chocolate, or a card." He tilted his head. "Maybe flowers, chocolate, and a card could help. Is there a 'sorry I'm an asshole' card?"

His dumb schemes gave me an idea. "I think I know what to do," I said.

"Oh, great, if you're going with my idea, you're totally doomed." He picked up one of the coffee mugs and took a sip. A second later, he pulled the cup away and hissed air between his front teeth. "This shit's hot."

"It's coffee."

I wasn't going to go with flowers, chocolate, or a card. I had a better idea, a crazy idea, but a better one than his. Maybe she wouldn't want me back, and if that were true, I'd leave her be, but I hoped there was still a chance to fix what I'd broken.

CHAPTER TWENTY-TWO

KANDRA

With a small smile at the little nursery, I absentmindedly rubbed my flat belly while thinking about the crib I ordered. It would arrive in a few weeks, and I couldn't wait.

Now that my secret was out, I figured I might as well start getting ready. Although the room was mostly blank, I could envision it all set up. There was a cute comforter online that I'd come back to again and again. It was decorated with happy little animals. If it made me smile in my darkest hours, then surely it would be pleasant for the baby.

Even with a heavy heart, I was determined to make the best of my situation. While it was humiliating to know that the whole world knew my secret, it was also kind of a relief.

I ran my fingertip along the bookshelf, thinking about Noah. I'd done my best to exile him from my thoughts, but he crept back in more often than I'd like to admit. I wasn't mad at him, and I didn't hate him. I was the one who screwed up, and I couldn't fault him for being upset and breaking things off.

I accepted the facts, but that didn't mean they stopped hurting.

I blinked back tears as my doorbell rang. With a sigh, I lumbered toward the door. That would be my mother with coffee and likely disappointed words. I put her off for a day but knew I needed to talk to her. With a heavy heart, I opened the front door.

Mom offered me my favorite coffee—but decaf because she's my mother and there was no way she'd let me drink caffeine while pregnant. I took it with a soft thank you and stepped inside, but not before I saw the sadness in her eyes and the tiny anguished smile tugging the corners of her lips.

I took a sip of my sweet vanilla latte and sat on the couch. She followed and took the cushion beside me. "I don't have a lot of time," she said, and I tilted my head at her, surprised.

"I thought it would be better if I kept this short and sweet, anyway."

She put her hand on mine and leaned in a little closer. "I'm not mad, nor am I disappointed in you. Kandra, I love you. Why didn't you tell me?"

"Oh, Mom. Your last words to me were not to get knocked up. You had dreams for me, and I had them for myself. Yet here I am, back in Cross Creek, broke and pregnant." I blinked back tears as her eyes locked on mine.

"I could never be upset with you. You're my daughter." Her hand settled on my stomach. "What better accomplishment is there than to have a child? They are the gift that keeps giving." She sat back and clapped her hands. "And I'm going to be a grandmother, and I don't think anything could be as exciting as that."

"I'm sorry you had to find out the way you did."

"I could just kill Benji … he was wrong to do this." Anger colored her tone, and fire ignited in her eyes as she spoke. "He had no right to say and do those things." She took a deep breath before continuing in her kind, warm voice that soothed the painful parts of my soul like a balm. "You're an adult, sweet pea. Life is hard, and there's no manual. We just have to do our best, and I trust you're doing exactly that."

All the things I wanted to say melted away in the face of her overwhelming support. She stood up and gently tugged my hand. I got to my feet, and she held me in a tight hug that left me breathlessly happy.

"I love you, sweet pea. No matter what." She stepped back and brushed my hair out of my face. "You tell me what I can do, and I'll help in any way you ask. Or I can let you be. Whatever you wish, but know that I love you, and I already love my grandchild." With that, she planted a kiss on my forehead, beamed at me, and gave my cheek a gentle pinch.

I smiled through the threatening thunderstorm of emotions. This was not the talk I envisioned, but it was the talk I needed more than anything.

"Now, I've got to run." She hesitated, then stared at me for a second, her eyes searching my face. "Unless you need me to stay."

She was willing to cancel whatever she had planned to be here with me. The thought warmed me up, and I wanted to hug myself happily. Instead, I waved her off with a smile. "Go! I'll call you later."

I showed her to the door with my coffee in hand and a big, stupid grin on my face. Despite the pain echoing through me, there was joy there too, and love I desperately needed. As she got into her little SUV and pulled away from the curb, a red car entered my driveway. Mom honked and waved at the driver, and I tried to see through the sun glaring on the windshield to figure out who it was.

I couldn't tell and sipped my coffee, trying to relax. Surely it was just someone coming by to say hello, but what if it wasn't? What if it was Anthony and he'd changed his mind? I'd never let him into my life again, but could I keep him from his child? I shook the thought from my mind because Anthony was a child, and there was no way he could raise one.

The driver's side door opened, and a woman stepped out. Sunglasses covered her eyes and long brown hair tumbled down her back as she closed the door behind her. She slung a purse over her shoulder before heading my way with open arms.

"Kandra!"

I'd recognize that voice anywhere. "Melanie?" We were best friends in high school, and she left Cross Creek when I did. Though we'd been in contact regularly, I hadn't touched base with her since my move back home. How many times had I wanted to call her? "What are you doing in Cross Creek?"

She walked right up and tugged me to her chest. "Obligatory parental visit. It's like bad medicine; you swallow it fast and hope it goes down easy." As she rocked me side to side and squeezed me tightly, she hummed low in her throat. "I missed you so much, woman." She pressed a kiss to my cheek and backed up a step.

"Come on in," I said, leading her inside. "Want coffee or something else to drink?"

She shook her head. "I'm on a caffeine break. It sucks, but doc wants me to try." Pulling her glasses off, she looked me up and down like she suspected something. "How are you?"

"I'm good." How much could she possibly know? "Who told you I was here?"

"You know, nothing stays a secret for long."

That was the truth.

"Time to catch up." She dug her toe into one heel, slipped the shoe off, and then did the same on the other side before plopping down on the couch. She folded her legs up under her and stared at me expectantly. Her black athletic pants fit her like a glove, and her tank top showed off her sports bra. She looked like she'd been out for a run, but that was just her style.

"Noah and I tried again, but I didn't tell him I'm pregnant

with Anthony's baby, and Benji found out, blurted it in the diner, and wrote an exposé on me. That's how Noah found out about the baby, and he dumped me." The words just poured out. After I finished talking, silence followed.

She scowled.

"Wait..." With a little shake of her head, she seemed to try to clear her mind and get all the facts in order. "You and Noah, again?"

I nodded, swallowing hard.

"And you're pregnant? With Anthony's baby?"

I nodded again.

Her serious expression tightened. "I could hurt Benji. Do you have a baseball bat?"

I couldn't hold back a giggle. "You're not attacking Benji with a baseball bat."

"He wrote an article on you? Seriously? That's just wrong." Her lip curled, and she pulled me into a quick hug before letting me go. "He's trash."

I didn't disagree, so I stayed quiet.

"I can't believe Noah dumped you." She sat back like the weight of those thoughts crushed her into the couch.

I shrugged. "I deserved it. I didn't come clean and tell him right away, and I should have."

She went silent a moment and said, "Luckily, you're strong and don't need a man."

That wasn't the point. I knew I was strong, and I knew I could do this on my own, but I didn't *want* to. I wanted Noah at my side. Not just for help, but because I loved him. I wanted him next to me to celebrate every victory, to mourn every loss, and to share every experience. I was a fool to leave all those years ago. I got caught up in the wonder and excitement of it all, and look where it got me. I was back in Cross Creek with less than I left with. It was a great lesson in the old adage that the grass was greener on the other side. In my case, the grass was greener because it was artificial turf. In the end, I had to leave and learn and grow to realize how much I'd left behind. Hindsight is always twenty-twenty.

Now that I was back, I could clearly see what I'd given up. Every bit of the adult me believed that Noah was the right guy for me; I wanted a partner, an equal. I wanted a man I could walk beside, not behind. Noah was confident enough not to be threatened by my need to have power and control over my life. But ... I screwed up and ruined what we could have had, and now I'd walk my path alone.

"So, what are you going to do?" Her eyes locked on me, and the heavy question seemed to trouble her.

I lifted my shoulders. "I'm having a baby."

"You'll get child support from Anthony, right?" Her tone held more than a hint of disgust for my ex, but I'd made my peace with him being out of my life.

When I shook my head, she sat upright. "Why not? He helped make this baby, and he can help support it."

That wasn't the point. "I don't want to have to deal with him. I'm not afraid of him or anything, but I'd rather not have the extra stress in my life, you know? He didn't want anything to do with me or this baby, and I'm not about to force him to be a part of our lives." He wasn't worth the space of a thought in my mind.

That seemed to make sense to her, and she sat back in her seat again.

I took a drink of my coffee, loving the flavor.

"Do you want Noah back?" Her green eyes met mine, and she sat up and studied me carefully.

I nodded. "I do, but that bridge is burned, and there's no rebuilding it now."

"You love him, don't you?" Her question hit my heart like an arrow.

Unable to speak, I simply nodded. It didn't matter that I loved

Noah. I'd messed up, and it was over. I'd come to terms with that already.

"Oh, hon." She leaned in and gave me another hug. With a quick pat on my shoulder, she pulled away, and I tried to smile through my pain.

"Want to see the nursery? It's not done, but I ordered the crib and can show you where I'll put it." I wanted to shift the topic to less painful things, though I didn't doubt Noah would linger in my mind for far longer than I wanted him to.

She jumped to her feet and followed me into the room. With a happy little sound, she glanced at the rocking chair I'd positioned under the window beside the bookshelf and turned to me. "What color are you painting the room?"

"Not sure yet." My heart lifted as I looked around the bright, airy space. "I don't know if I'm having a boy or a girl."

She didn't seem surprised as she ran her hand over the bookshelf Noah and I had built together. "I figured you would have told me already if you knew. Or are you keeping it a secret?"

I could hardly focus on what she was asking as the memory of Noah and me laughing over bookshelf directions filled my thoughts. As the realization that he would never help me set up another thing crept in, sadness followed. It was over between us, and that broke my heart.

"Nope, no more secrets."

CHAPTER TWENTY-THREE

NOAH

With the phone to my ear, I smiled. A real smile that I felt to my bones. Two weeks had passed since I'd broken things off with Kandra. They were the longest two weeks of my life, but I'd finally made a decision—a decision to change everything. All the parts were already in motion, and all I had to do was the legwork.

"I know, Mom," I said.

"I love you, young man." Despite the stern edge in her voice, I could hear the pride and affection there too. "Your father would be so proud of you."

"Thank you." I blinked back the moisture in my eyes and tilted my head to stare at the ceiling. Tracing the heavy wooden beams of my home, I sighed.

"Good luck. I have a feeling you'll need it."

"I hope I don't need it, but thanks." We said our goodbyes, and I hung up the phone. Most of the weight had lifted off my shoulders, and new hope sprung to life inside me. As I glanced around my home, my gaze settled on the couch, and memories of Dad filled my mind.

I could almost hear his voice. *I know you love her son, but sometimes people need time and space. Maybe she'll come back one day. Maybe she never will. Whatever happens, will happen, but you need to make sure you're a good man no matter what.*

My eyes misted over as I glanced at the backyard and saw us tossing a baseball back and forth. *It's a nice place you have here. Trust me, it's not easy for your mother or me to watch you boys grow up and leave the house one by one, but we're so proud of you.*

I wandered through the house, guided by his voice, by the memories I had of him visiting before the universe so cruelly stole him away. Stopping in the kitchen, I glanced at the stove hood we'd pulled out, repaired, and replaced.

You don't need my help, he said, calling me out on my bullshit.

He was right and wrong. "Of course, I need you, Dad. It's nice to have time with you." I mouthed the words in the quiet space as I remembered him handing me tools and offering advice while we worked.

I hadn't just moved out and gone about my life. I'd kept him and Mom near, but Dad was the pillar of strength in my life. He was the beacon of the type of man I wanted to be. He was patient and kind, quick to laugh, and always there for those he loved. He knew how to cheer someone up and had the best wisdom when it was needed most.

Wandering into the backyard, I took in the grill, and I swore I could see him there. *Are you sure you want me to grill at your house?* He'd asked.

I knew how much he loved to grill, and I'd picked up a nice one for him to enjoy when he and Mom came over for dinner.

As my attention drifted, I saw him telling me where I could put the hot tub a few months before he passed.

I stood on the grass in the middle of the yard and turned to walk inside. In the doorway, I saw the memory of the last time he visited. I could feel him pull me into a warm hug. *It's been too long; I've missed you. I thought we could go fishing today.*

With a bittersweet, painful smile, I closed the door and locked it.

IN FRONT of Kandra's door, I hesitated. I wasn't sure why. Maybe it was the red car out front. Who's was it? Did I have a right to know—to care? Was it fear? Maybe. Was I worried she wouldn't want to see me? Sure. Did I regret the choices I'd made in the last two weeks? Not one bit. With a slightly unsteady hand, I rang her doorbell.

The floor creaked as she approached the door. I caught myself holding my breath, letting it out, and then pulling in another while I waited to see if she would open the door for me.

A heartbeat later, she cracked it but blocked the entrance with her body. "What's up?" she asked coolly, her beautiful eyes on mine.

"Can we talk?" I wiped my sweaty palms on my pants. This woman had me as nervous as a teenaged boy again. Kandra was the only woman who had ever made me feel like that.

Panic lit in her eyes, and she shifted the door slightly as if she was about to close it in my face. For a moment, we stood there, a pause between us while she seemed to struggle internally about letting me in. Just when I was sure she'd send me away, the vulnerability in her eyes caught my attention and jealous anger buzzed in my gut.

Was the red car Anthony's? Had he come to his senses and came back to her? Did he have a change of heart and decide he wanted her after all? Was I too late to save the spark between us and win her back?

My heart sank as the thought that the things I'd done in the last two weeks had been for nothing.

I glanced past her and saw it wasn't Anthony at all. No, it was her friend Melanie. I'd thought Melanie moved away from Cross Creek; had she come back?

"Hey, Noah," Melanie said in an icy tone as she walked toward Kandra.

"Hello," I rubbed at the back of my neck. I thought it was Anthony, and I'd been jealous. Angry even, and so afraid to lose Kandra.

Mel kissed Kandra's cheek and spoke softly. "I'll be at my parents' house if you need me, and don't forget what I told you." With that, she slipped past me, out the front door, without so much as another look in my direction.

What had she told Kandra that was important for her not to forget? Those two were best friends back in the day, and Mel was always a good person and a good influence. Kandra trusted her.

I turned to look back at Kandra, only to find the door open and empty. Was it an invitation to come in? Why else would she have left the door open and walked away?

"Can I come in?"

With her back to me, she nodded, and I breathed a sigh of relief. Stepping inside, I closed the door behind me and turned to face her. She still had her back to me, and I sensed she was getting her bearings. When she turned around, her arms crossed her belly protectively, and my heart ached as I thought about her gearing up to protect herself from me.

Do you think I'd hurt you? I'd asked her not so long ago.

Not physically, she'd said in such a soulful, honest tone that it tore my heart to shreds. Now she was gearing up for more pain from me, and it stung. What was worse was I knew I deserved it because I hurt her, and I regretted that with every ounce of my being.

"I want to say I'm sorry."

Her shoulders straightened, but she made no other indication she heard me. I didn't mind if she wouldn't look at me, because I knew she was listening to my words, and I planned to deliver them wisely.

"I've been fumbling through my whole life. I haven't had a solid relationship since you left the first time." I let out a nervous chuckle and raked my fingers through my hair before taking a step closer. I wanted to reach out, touch her shoulder, pull her into a hug, inhale her sweet scent, and kiss her soft cheek. "I know why now. It's always been you. I've never been serious about anyone else because deep down, I've always known you were the one for me. If I couldn't have you, I wouldn't have anyone."

I took another step forward. I was so close I could almost touch her, but I didn't. "I want you in my life, and I finally figured it out. For that to happen, I need to accept everything about you. I need to embrace your joys, your heartbreaks, and your pregnancy ... if you're willing to share them with me." I added that last part as doubt crept in because she still wasn't looking at me.

Maybe this wasn't going to work. I'd been deliberately cruel to her. Was I too late to fix this?

Reaching out, I gently touched her shoulders, and she turned and lifted her chin to face me. Tears streamed down her cheeks. Every bit I had been holding back broke, and I pulled her into my arms, wrapping her into a hug. Stroking her hair, I lowered my lips to her head and whispered another apology for hurting her and for being a dick and for screwing everything up so badly.

"I want to make it right, and for the past two weeks, I've been making plans." My heart leaped. "I bought a home for us. The one we saw when we were horseback riding." I squeezed my eyes closed as I thought about how I had to give up my current home and all its memories of Dad to make this purchase.

I'd still have those memories, even if I didn't have the place they were tied to. So why did it hurt so bad? With a deep breath, I reminded myself that she was worth it. She didn't know any of that, and she didn't need to know what I was giving up for our fresh start.

"It needs some work, but I thought we could fix it up together." My best memories of Dad in my home were of us restoring the place. I could imagine building those kinds of memories with Kandra in our new place. "It came with a few acres and we have access to the creek." It was the creek we played in as kids, though in a different spot. "It's a wonderful place for a child to grow up."

I wanted her to know I'd done all of this with the hopes of us becoming a family in the back of my mind. "But there's something I have to ask you first," I hoped her silence was stunned surprise or joy. Letting her go, I knelt down for the second time and again took a little box out of my pocket. This time feeling like we were both in the same place and wanted the same things.

"I'm an asshole, but I'm the asshole that's been in love with you from the beginning. I'll make mistakes, but I'll try to be worthy of you. I want you with me now and forever. I know before the timing wasn't right, and we both needed to do some soul-searching, but I want to ask you now, will you marry me?"

Her body stiffened, and her eyes met mine. *So not the reaction I expected this time, but I'm gonna let her explain.*

"Whoa, what happened? Are you okay? What's wrong?" I stood up and tucked the box back into my pocket, my mind solely on her well-being.

"You just thought you could say sorry, and everything would be perfect? Really? When Benji told the entire diner I was trying to trick you into being my baby's father, do you have any idea how hurt I was? I thought for sure you would defend me and tell everyone that I would never do something like that. I thought you of all people knew my character, yet you didn't. You didn't even comfort me. And now you made all these decisions without me? You bought a house and thought what?"

My heart sank. Everything with the house was final. I dropped my keys off on the way here. I no longer owned my home, but now owned a house on the creek where it looked like I'd live alone.

"You just assumed I'd be happy to get to move in with you, and you didn't bother talking to me first. That's not what a relationship is supposed to look like." Her hand trembled as she shoved her hair back from her face. "I told you I want to be your partner—your equal. That means we make decisions together."

She had a valid point. Maybe I jumped the gun. This idea was way better in my head. *I guess it's true about assumptions ... I'm a total ass.*

CHAPTER TWENTY-FOUR

KANDRA

"Noah, I can't marry you. I can't marry anyone who doesn't value me or my opinion." I took a deep breath and realized the words I said weren't the words I meant to say, but before I could amend my statement, I noticed the hurt in his eyes, and it hit me like a mule kick to the gut squeezing the air out of my lungs.

Did I mean it? How did we end up here again? With every second that ticked by, my chances of clearing this up grew slimmer and slimmer.

His lips parted, but he said nothing as he studied me. Then his whole expression wiped blank. All the hurt, all the confusion and surprise vanished, replaced by something colder than ice.

I was losing him, or maybe I'd already lost him.

"I don't want you to marry me because you think you have to take care of me." The words finally began to leave my pinched throat. "I don't want you making life-changing decisions for both of us without consulting me. I don't want to be your passenger in life; I want to be a copilot."

His Adam's apple lifted, then slid down an inch. I took a step back and folded one arm across my ribs, the other hand I placed at my throat. The thundering of my pulse startled me.

"I don't need you to save me or my baby. I'll figure things out on my own. I have my mother's support. I have friends. I have options." I'd save myself, thank you very much. I could afford my own place. I could do this! I didn't need him to feel bad or for him to do what he thought was the right thing.

He told me he loved me. He apologized for being cruel and dumping me, though I wanted him to know I didn't see it that way.

"You aren't a dick for dumping me. I didn't tell you something I should have confessed early on." I still believed that, regardless of what Melanie had said or what my mother thought. Being with someone meant being open and honest with them, even when it was uncomfortable.

He told me he was fumbling through his whole life, and he hadn't been serious about anyone since me. He said I was the one for him, but what if his love was skewed with worry and pity and a need to take care of me? Noah was a protector at his core. He always had been. He'd do whatever it took to keep me safe. But did he believe me when I said I didn't need to be saved? Did he understand my need to be equal? Did he trust that I could do this on my own?

I studied his impassive features.

"I want a partner." I lowered my voice and traced his face with my gaze, aware this might be turning into our final goodbye. The thought shattered me, and I inhaled past the lump in my throat. "I want a friend and a lover. I don't just want a dad for my child, because if that's the only reason you want me, then everything will fall apart."

I needed him to understand. Taking another step closer, I took his hands in mine and looked into his eyes. "I know you want to protect me, Noah. You always have, and I love that about you, but you don't need to this time. I'll be okay."

To my horror, his perfectly calm mask broke, and he laughed.

"Do you think," he asked in a warmer tone than I ever expected, "that I'm only asking you to marry me because I need to save you or because I want your baby to have a father? Do you think I said I love you because of some twisted sense of honor or duty?"

He cocked his head and waited.

"Well, it obviously crossed my mind." I lifted both shoulders, aware I wasn't sure if this was his reason. "I need to know that saving me isn't a motivating factor. You think you need to buy me houses, accept my pregnancy, and take care of me, and that's worrisome."

He chuckled. "Sorry, I'm not trying to be a dick, and I'm not laughing at you."

"Sure feels like it," I muttered, a bit of humor creeping into my aching heart.

He let go of my hands and grabbed my shoulders as I peeked up at him. "I'm laughing at the thought of you needing anyone to take care of you. I know how strong you are."

He gave my shoulders a squeeze.

"And when I think about you putting Benji in his place despite your hatred of being humiliated in public…" He laughed again, and I couldn't hold back a grin. I had torn into Benji pretty good.

"I think you broke him. I mean, he published the article, but he only did it because he couldn't back down after the verbal whipping you gave him." He pulled me into his arms. "I'm sorry for doing something without your approval, but I swear it came from a good place."

I melted into his arms and clung to him.

"I'm sorry too." I buried my face in his chest and breathed him in.

"I do see you as an equal, and as a partner." He tipped my chin back with his thumb. "As a friend and a lover too. I messed up. Can I make it up to you? I'm not going to give up on us that easily."

My stomach dipped.

He continued. "I already lost you twice, and I'm not letting it happen again." His eyes bore into mine, and I couldn't hold back my words.

"Sounds like you've made up your mind."

He must have detected the humor in my voice because he arched a brow and smiled. "I see you as a partner, but I'm also willing to do whatever it takes to make everything right between us. If you want me to go, I will, but if there is anything I can do—"

"Yes," I blurted.

His brows furrowed, leaving a crease in the center of his forehead. It was as if he didn't understand what I was saying.

I sure as heck wasn't going to give it to him easily. An evil grin crossed my lips. "Yes."

"Yes, there's something I can do?" He stared at me. "Sure, I'll do it, just tell me."

Instead, I simply said, "Yes!" with more volume and enthusiasm.

"I think I'm missing something." He studied my face, clearly searching for answers.

Maybe it was time to take pity on the poor guy. We could figure out the details later. For now, I knew one thing for certain. I would marry Noah Lockhart. "Yes, Noah, I'll marry you."

His eyes lit up, and he lowered his lips to mine.

His mouth moved to touch my forehead, and he gave me a gentle squeeze that echoed the surge of joy in my heart. He lowered to one knee and pulled out the box again.

"It's not a diamond; it's a white sapphire." He opened the box, and I gasped at the stunning stone. The thin rose gold band was crusted with tiny diamonds, but the white sapphire set in the center was incredible.

"It's the most beautiful ring I've ever seen," I whispered, my eyes misting over. It was perfect. Somehow he knew me better than I knew myself.

With a smile, he slipped it on my finger before standing up and pressing another quick kiss to my lips.

"Did you really buy us that house?" Nothing about our conversation seemed real. It had to be a dream, and pretty soon, Melanie would smack me across the face and pull me out of this amazingly crazy fantasy. As deliriously happy as I was, I wasn't totally on board with moving out of my home.

This was the place I used to prove that I didn't need Anthony's help. It was a house I'd built into a home—a safe space to hide when I was weary of the world.

"Are you okay?" he asked.

I nodded, still struggling. Wasn't this supposed to be an easy choice? I loved and trusted Noah. Still, my freedom was important after everything I'd gone through with Anthony. Was I punishing Noah for Anthony's mistakes?

I needed to sleep on it and not make any rash decisions or hasty plans.

"Oh! I have something for you!" I pulled away and ran into my room as I remembered the gift. Picking up the picture of Noah and his father, I smiled. They'd been watching me from my nightstand every day since I found the picture and frame. I'd taken the image of father and son long ago, and I'd printed it and framed it.

I promised myself I'd give it to him for his birthday, but now I didn't have to wait. I pressed it to my belly and carried it out to Noah. His eyes lit up as he watched me walk toward him. I stopped in front of him and sighed.

I held out the image, and he took it gingerly, a confused look crossed his face. "Where did you get this?"

"I found it on one of my memory cards."

He looked at the image of him and his father, and his features went white.

"Noah, what's wrong?" I reached out to touch his shoulder, and he looked at me.

"This is the best gift I could ever imagine receiving," he said, his voice thick as I held him in a tight embrace. "I forgot about this picture."

Suddenly the sweet gesture felt bittersweet. "I'm sorry for bringing all of that back, and I'm sorry he's gone." His dad was such a wonderful man.

"Please, don't be sorry." He nestled his chin against my shoulder, and I was sure he was staring at the image over it, soaking in every detail of that summer day. "I mean it, this is incredible. I love you."

"I love you, too," I said, still hugging him tightly.

I was going to make sure I showed him my love every chance I had starting right now. There were no guarantees of how much time we'd have together, no promises of long lives, or tomorrows, so I vowed to make sure every second counted. I already wasted so many years, looking for something that was right in front of me all along. Noah's all-consuming love is my heart's true north, and I will never lose sight of that again.

CHAPTER 25
NOAH

I glanced over my shoulder to see Kandra sitting next to Quinn and sipping a glass of water. I smiled as he talked to her with animated features and expressive hands, but I couldn't make out his words. Her gaze met mine, and the corners of her lips curved up as she lingered on me.

Bayden ignored Quinn as he squeezed the juice of half a lemon on his thyme-roasted carrot dish, and Ethan slipped rolls in with the shepherd's pie that was beginning to brown on top.

"Five minutes?" I asked them.

"Eight," Ethan said, and Bayden nodded in agreement.

I slipped over to Kandra and wrapped an arm around her shoulders. Quinn didn't even take a breath. "And then he walked right into a pole."

I knew the story well. At sixteen, Ethan had been so in love with a girl that while he was walking and looking at her, he'd slammed face-first into a pole. Needless to say, she hadn't been interested in dating the clumsy oaf.

"I should get back to the table," Kandra said as I rubbed her lower back. She'd been in some pain, and her belly left me wanting to rub her like a magic lamp, but when she said she needed to go, I knew that meant she needed to sit somewhere more comfortable. I took her hand and kept an arm wrapped around her and helped support her weight into the dining room.

"Are you okay?" My mother's worried tone earned a smile from Kandra.

"I'm sore, tired, and a bit achy, but I'm okay." She settled into the chair with a grateful glance at me, and I pressed a quick kiss to her lips before speaking.

"How's the house coming?" Mom asked.

We were living in Kandra's rental until the renovations were done on our place, but it didn't matter where we lived as long as we were together.

Looking at my wife, I saw that hungry, I-could-eat-a-bear look on her face. "About six minutes left on dinner," I said.

"Seven!" Ethan called out, and I rolled my eyes.

"It's been more than a minute!" I said as the women swapped knowing glances. "Love you." I touched Kandra's cheek before heading back into the kitchen.

A quick peek in the oven told me the shepherd's pie was done, and I grabbed potholders. Carrying the dish to the table, I set it down, and almost bumped into Bayden as he brought his carrots to the table.

"The rolls aren't done!" Ethan's frustration shone in his voice.

"It's fine," Mom spoke up, and the tension in the room eased.

"Do you want anything else to drink?" I asked Kandra, who shook her head. A few moments later, Ethan popped out of the kitchen with hot rolls. Quinn brought the butter, honey, and utensils as we all gathered around the table. I sat beside Kandra and took a moment looking at Dad's empty seat.

Quinn broke the silence. "So, how's Sheriff Miranda?" he asked Bayden, who fixed a death glare on him.

I stood up with a plate and pointed at things, my gaze catching

Kandra's. She nodded, and I piled food on her plate as my brothers stared at one another. Mom and Ethan dug in but watched Bayden and Quinn's showdown with curiosity.

I handed Kandra her food and grabbed my plate.

"How would I know?" Bayden finally asked.

"Well, I mean, you're in love with her, so you know how she's doing, right?" Quinn faked an innocent expression while piling food onto his plate.

Bayden's anger grew, and I imagined steam coming out of his ears and nose. If Quinn kept pushing, he might erupt. So, I threw gasoline on the fire.

"Are you going to be next?" I asked, showing off my wedding band.

Mom's smile grew as she watched the events unfold with a "boys will boys" expression. No doubt, she knew by now there was no stopping us.

A loud ringtone cut through the silence, and Bayden pulled out his phone. Quinn took the opportunity to snatch it before dashing from the table.

"It's Miranda!" he said, holding the phone up with a triumphant grin. Then he glanced at it again. "Wait, she's calling you?" He handed the phone back to Bayden, who touched the red icon and went back to his food.

"Why didn't you answer?" Ethan lifted a bite to his mouth as Kandra stretched her legs out across my lap. I absentmindedly rubbed her swollen ankles while I ate a carrot.

"None of your business." Bayden was done with our crap. "Now, leave me alone."

Quinn and Ethan glanced at each other, and Kandra giggled.

"They're in love," Quinn said. Ethan nodded in agreement, and Mom snorted.

"So, you are next," I said to Bayden, who gave me a sullen look before taking a bite of his food. I glanced over and noticed Kandra was on her last bite and smiled at her.

"More?" I asked.

She sighed, her eyes widening as she met my gaze. "Not yet," she said softly, rubbing her belly with both hands. Before I could react, she grabbed Mom's hand and put it on her stomach. "The baby's kicking."

My brothers crowded around and waited for permission to touch while I watched, adoring my wife and the way she glowed. They felt the baby move, and their faces lit up.

Even Bayden seemed to relax as the tiny one kicked his hand. I held back, aware that it was a joy I got to experience often, but it was reasonably new to my brothers. I couldn't wait to be a father, and I was excited to introduce our baby to the world.

Kandra addressed Bayden as Ethan and Quinn moved back to their seats. "I bet Miranda would be cute pregnant."

Quinn fell out of his chair, Ethan burst out laughing, and Bayden's face went red. Mom covered her mouth and stared at Bayden, who actually smiled.

He freaking smiled when she teased him.

"You've thought about it!" Kandra's surprised tone and the look on Bayden's face said she'd nailed it right on the head. "Oh, honey, you better make a move. She's a wonderful, beautiful person, and you'll never forgive yourself if you miss your shot with her."

He gave the barest hint of a nod, and I sat there, stunned. Of all of us, it was Kandra that got through to him? As shocked as I was, I was also impressed and secretly thrilled. Maybe now he would get serious about the pretty sheriff and try to build something worthwhile with her. We could hope, at least. The two would be great together, I just knew it.

He went back to his seat, refusing to look at the rest of us.

"Let's leave Bayden alone," Mom said before glancing at Quinn. "So how about you? Anyone special in your life?"

He shook his head.

Then Ethan shook his. "Me either, but I'm not in a hurry."

I finished my dinner while I watched them all talk. As much as I missed my time with Dad, I couldn't help but realize how incredibly lucky I was for moments like these. For family dinners. For family love, laughter, and teasing.

My brothers dug back into the food, and I looked at Kandra before nodding, asking her without words if she wanted more. She nodded with a big grin on her face.

I scooped up the shepherd's pie, proud of how well my dish had turned out. It wasn't officially a competition, but of course, my brothers and I treated it like one, and my meal was better than theirs, meaning I won. I needed to start stepping it up, though, because Bayden's cooking skills were improving. No way I could let him be better at it than I was.

I added carrots and a roll to Kandra's plate and passed it to her. She picked up the honey, split her roll, and dumped the sweet stuff on it. It was something she did and had gotten Ethan and Quinn stuck on. They'd never tried honey on rolls before, and now they were hooked. I admired her appetite, and given that she was growing a baby, she needed the extra calories.

"It's not like I'm actively trying not to meet someone," Quinn said to our mother while Bayden glanced at his phone under the edge of the table. I didn't doubt he was texting Miranda, given the grin on his face. She was the only one that made him smile like that. I hoped he would find love and that the battles would be few.

As Quinn and Ethan chatted with Mom about their sad lack of love lives, I watched Kandra. She watched them talk but caught my eye and flashed a slight smile that lit up my life. We were going to have our child any day now—*our* child.

I'd slipped up and said something to the effect of *you're having my baby* while we argued about her climbing a stepladder. I'd been so afraid she might fall that the words slipped out along with some variation of I'd never forgive myself if you got hurt. She'd smiled, then said, *your baby?* Ever since then, I said my baby or our baby, and I stood by that. I would love the child as my own. In fact, I already did. I didn't give a shit who donated the sperm. I would be present and teach the little one to ride a bike and fish. It would be me showing him how to be a good man if he were a boy and demand a good partner if she were a girl. Scratch that, if it was a she, I wouldn't let her out of the house until she was thirty.

"You okay?" Kandra asked.

"Couldn't be better." Surrounded by family, I realized I only had one regret and that was that Dad wasn't here. He would love every second of this. He'd relish the joy and love.

I glanced at his picture, one similar to the one Kandra gave me. She printed a photo of Dad for everyone in the family, and now he sat, watching us eat dinner, his smile warming the room. For a moment, I swore I could hear his voice.

I've missed you. It's been too long.

I glanced at my wife, joy flooding every inch of my being. My life was full to bursting and better than I could have ever imagined.

I was once broken and wasn't sure if I would ever be whole again, but with Kandra by my side, I was finally complete. I didn't doubt that my father knew it, that he was happy for me, and that he was smiling on us from wherever he was.

I touched Kandra's belly and smiled as the little one pushed back.

Life was perfect in Cross Creek. It was a town with a population of 2,500 people, and I couldn't get enough of the five I loved the most.

Do you want to read a deleted/bonus scene?

Click here.

SNEAK PEEK AT FEARLESS HART
MIRANDA

I didn't drive the old back roads because they reminded me of where I'd grown up and memories I wasn't ready to face; memories I'd fled to Cross Creek to escape.

But the funny thing about the past is that it has a way of following no matter how far or fast you run.

My Tahoe's headlights danced as my tires hit three potholes, perfectly staggered to be impossible to miss.

"Damn it," I growled as my water bottle popped out of the cup holder to roll around on the passenger floor, well out of reach. Not that I'd be so irresponsible as to reach for it while I was driving.

I wouldn't even be on this bumpy-ass road if I hadn't received a report that someone was on an old farm out here. A neighbor called in a suspicious vehicle, and though there was little to no crime in Cross Creek, I still needed to check it out. Nothing got past the old folks in this town. They might have been deaf, but they heard everything; blind but somehow could see a trespasser from a mile away.

No doubt I'd probably just come across teens making out and send them on their way. I'd already heard from dispatch that Ethel tried to talk her ear off while making the call, and I smiled as I thought about the sweet old couple. Still, I breathed a sigh of relief that the call was over trespassers and not more drama from Benji, the town journalist, who took it upon himself to air everyone else's dirty laundry. Publishing that article about Kandra's personal life was just bad journalism counting on sensationalism, and it almost broke Kandra and Noah up.

Hitting the brakes, I waited for two deer who entered the road. They stopped mid-lane, staring at me before bolting across the street into the field's chest-high grass.

I watched them go while my thoughts wandered back to how Benji would get out of this trouble. Something about him set off my alarm bells a long time ago. But what he'd done to Kandra was downright predatory, and the entire town saw it and rallied behind her.

Just last week, there had been a town-wide baby shower for the mom-to-be, and she and Noah were guests of honor. Everyone showed up and brought more things than one child could ever use or need.

An event like that told me exactly what kind of town I lived in. On the flip side, Benji had found himself persona non grata. Even Roy booted him, which meant I could go to the bar for a beer to unwind without the nosy journalist bugging me for an interview.

"Good riddance." The sound of my voice echoed through the cab of the cruiser. "I don't want him digging into my past for dirt because my life is a damn landfill."

The old farmhouse loomed to my right, rising like an ethereal ghost through the layer of fog drifting in from the creek. A truck came into view, and I chuckled. Things were about to get more interesting. I hadn't stumbled upon kids making out after all.

My pulse was racing as I parked. Trying to steady it, I scooped my water bottle off the passenger floor and took a long drink before exiting my vehicle.

My eyes adjusted to the total darkness while I moved to the truck. Overhead, a billion stars shone like an impossible scattering of fairy lights. The moon added a silvery glow as my breath hung in mini clouds near my face.

The dark mixed with the night lit up by stars, and the left behind fog gave the whole place an almost spooky feel as I approached Bayden's form. That curious warmth he evoked in me didn't escape my notice, and I wondered if I was developing feelings because of how much we talked. I mean, he was part of the crew building the new police station. We consulted quite a lot, so the time we spent together would lead to a kind of closeness, right?

Maybe that was what I told myself to keep from panicking over feeling something toward someone. Relationships were not my superpower, and I avoided them like the plague.

"Am I going to have to cuff you?" I tucked my thumbs into my service belt and stopped a few feet away from him.

He chuckled. "Is that what you're into, Sheriff?" His husky tone sent a shiver down my spine.

"Risky question." I took a few steps closer to where the dirt road gave way to open fields of tall grass that danced in the sudden breeze. "It could end well for you, or you could wind up in the drunk tank." I arched an eyebrow at him.

He turned to face me, his handsome features clothed in an interesting mix of low light and deep shadows.

"What makes you think one of those isn't ending well for me?" His devilish grin broke me, and I let out a laugh.

"I guess if that's what you like, I can oblige." I reached for my cuffs, and he lifted both hands in mock surrender. "But really, why are you out here?"

"Did Ethel call me in?" he asked, sounding unfazed.

I shifted my weight and scanned the field as the wind

continued to toy with the dry grass. "Now isn't the time to be dodgy."

"Of course, she did." He let out a chuckle.

It didn't matter who had called him in; he was missing the point. "You're not supposed to be out here."

"I'm sorry, but it's a good place to think, and it's abandoned. I didn't mean any harm." He ran a hand through his dark hair, his body language still open and approachable despite the slight show of nerves.

The raw honesty of his words made me pause, and I swapped my sheriff's hat for my friend hat, the same way I would for anyone showing signs of distress. "What's on your mind?" I moved to stand shoulder to shoulder with him as he angled his body toward the old farmhouse. Under the moon's light, I saw the disrepair, the side panels falling away from the walls, the broken windows, the moss taking over an entire corner of the building.

"My dad built this place. It was his first real project. It was a passion project; off the books." His reflective tone drew the heart right out of my chest. "When I'm out here, I feel closer to him."

I nodded because there was nothing I needed to say. I'd stand there with Bayden for a few moments.

"But I'm ready to go," he mumbled with a sideways glance at me.

"I can give you a ride back." I lifted my shoulders, unsure if he was in any condition to drive.

He hesitated, then nodded. "That would be great. I'll have one of my brothers bring me back out tomorrow to get my truck."

"Noted," I said with a smile as we walked back toward my Tahoe.

On the way back, I took the surprise potholes more gently, though my water bottle still popped out of the holder. He caught the dark-blue bottle and tucked it back into its place.

"Thank you," I said.

He lifted a shoulder as if it was no big deal, but I hated the thing always escaping to crash around on the passenger floor. I'd been trying to fix it, but nothing had worked.

"Thank *you*," he said instead, staring out the window over the passing fields that enclosed the dirt road on both sides leading up to the old farmhouse. "For listening."

I sensed it was a struggle to open up and identified with that sentiment on more levels than I cared to admit. Sure, we talked, but it was never personal. Flirtatious? Yes. Intimate? No.

Before I could respond, he spoke up again. "And thanks, I guess, for not arresting me."

"You guess?" I said, arching an eyebrow at the road because there was no way I'd look at him.

"Well, there are worse things a beautiful woman could do to me, you know." I could imagine his panty-dropping smile, though I was immune—my panties weren't going anywhere.

If anyone else had said that, I'd be pissed. I'd feel like they were undermining my authority. But Bayden put me at ease, and our relaxed friendship had already proven he respected me far more than many people that blindly trusted me because of my badge. He didn't respect me out of obligation. He respected me because I'd proven I deserved his regard. There was a difference.

He angled his body toward me, tightening his belt as I pulled out onto the main highway. "Would you like to get a drink?" he asked in an even, hopeful tone.

I wanted to. I did. A beer sounded heavenly, but I shook my head no. "Can't, sorry. I'm on duty, and the city kind of frowns on officers drinking on the job."

"Where's your wild side—your sense of adventure?" He turned to stare at me. "Wait, the city only *kind of* frowns on it?"

He was something else.

I loved that he could make me laugh. I loved his quick humor and how easy he made our friendship. Despite the jokes and innuendo, which I was equally responsible for and an active participant most of the time, there were no expectations. There was no pressure. He was a friend, though the sexual attraction I had for him was anything but friendly.

Putting the brakes on those thoughts, I eased off the gas. No reason to speed on these roads in the dark. Not with the deer out and moving around under the light of the moon. Besides, I wasn't in a hurry since there wasn't much to do in a town with no actual crime.

"You're quiet tonight," he said.

I could feel his worried eyes studying me.

"It's Friday night, and I'm on a double shift." I usually worked twelve-hour shifts, but on Friday night, because of the occasional teen parties and minor issues like someone drinking too much and stumbling home, or even some random person trespassing at an old farmhouse, I worked a double.

"Need coffee?" He nodded at Roy's. Roy served coffee, but I wasn't sure I wanted to be seen in the bar.

"I can run in and grab you one to go if that helps."

On impulse, I pulled in, parked in a spot, and turned to him. "That sounds wonderful." I dug in my pocket, but he was out and gone before I could pull out my wallet. A few moments later, he was back with a steaming hot coffee in a cardboard to-go cup.

Bayden opened the door and got in. "Roy said he knows how you like it." He wiggled his eyebrows at me as the mouthwatering scent of—nonalcoholic—Irish cream and coffee met my nose.

"You're funny," I said, taking it and inhaling the steam before putting it in the cup holder on my side. I didn't like to put anything there because it was easy to bump with my knee, but I couldn't put it on his side where my water bottle was.

"Thanks."

I offered him money to pay for the coffee, and he stared at it, then at me as if I'd lost my mind. "I'm allowed to show my appreciation by buying an officer's coffee, right?"

I couldn't hold back a grin. "Thanks, but you don't have to do that."

"I know, but I want to." He buckled up, and I backed out and nosed the Tahoe toward his place with my heart feeling as warm as the coffee.

When I pulled in front of his house, I waited a second before speaking. "Try not to break the law, okay?"

He gave me a quick salute along with that cavalier grin that told me I hadn't seen the last of him before he climbed out of the SUV and headed toward his front door. I waited until he opened the door, worried about the melancholy attitude he had when I'd caught him at the old farm. He spun around in the doorway to face me with a warm smile on his face.

With a shake of my head, I pulled away from the curb. Bayden Lockhart was trouble, and I knew it.

GET A FREE BOOK.

Go to www.authorkellycollins.com

ABOUT THE AUTHOR

International bestselling author of more than thirty novels, Kelly Collins writes with the intention of keeping the love alive. Always a romantic, she blends real-life events with her vivid imagination to create characters and stories that lovers of contemporary romance, new adult, and romantic suspense will return to again and again.

For More Information
www.authorkellycollins.com
kelly@authorkellycollins.com